Casey's estranged husband is back.

Knowing Zach as she did, he probably wanted to talk about an amicable parting of the ways. Particularly since they had to work together. Well, she'd see about that. There was no way she could bear to see him every day.

Traffic slowed as Casey neared the hospital, and a new billboard caught her eye. At first she thought it was her imagination, but curiosity forced her to circle the block and drive by again.

Brilliant fuschia. Her favorite color.

I love you, Casey. Forgive me.

Casey couldn't get to the hospital staff parking lot fast enough. She slammed the door so hard it rocked the car. *Of all the nerve. He had to use my name. It wasn't enough that he left in the first place. No, he had to come back and make a public declaration. I'll be the laughingstock of the hospital.*

Well, the good doctor is going to find it isn't quite that easy. I'll find him if I have to look under every rock in the city, and when I do, he'll pay for playing me for a fool. I'll get to the bottom of this once and for all. Zachary Taylor has played enough games with my heart.

Her stride lengthened as she neared the staff lounge. Once inside, Casey dialed the office number from memory and got the answering service. *Desperate times call for desperate measures.* "I need to get an emergency message to Dr. Taylor."

TERRY FOWLER makes her home in North Carolina where she works for the city of Wilmington. The second oldest of five children, she shares a home with her best friend who is also her sister. Besides writing, her interests include genealogical research through the Internet and serving her small church in various activities.

Books by Terry Fowler

HEARTSONG PRESENTS
HP298—A Sense of Belonging

Double Take

Terry Fowler

Heartsong Presents

This book is dedicated to our Heavenly Father in loving appreciation for all the second chances He gives us and the blessings of family and friends.

Special thanks to Tammy and Gail for your assistance in getting the book completed and to Rebecca Germany for your valuable input.

A note from the author:
I love to hear from my readers! You may correspond with me by writing: **Terry Fowler**
Author Relations
PO Box 719
Uhrichsville, OH 44683

ISBN 1-57748-631-5

DOUBLE TAKE

Cover illustration by Kay Salem.

one

"That heartbreaking scoundrel is back!"

Casey Bordeaux-Taylor slapped the folded paper against the dashboard to emphasize her point.

"You can't be sure," her sister Stacey offered.

"*Slugger*," Casey emphasized. "Zach's 'mighty Casey' nickname."

"You aren't the only couple with nicknames for each other."

"It's Zach," Casey said confidently. "And I would be positive if you'd just make the call."

"The medical profession isn't the only one with a confidentiality clause."

"It's a classified ad," Casey muttered, "not a state secret. You manage the advertising department. Don't you approve the ads or something?"

Stacey braked for the yellow light and flashed her a "get real" look. "I wondered when I first saw it but decided it wasn't his style. Dr. Zachary Taylor wouldn't stoop to advertising his personal apologies. A lowlife like him couldn't be that romantic."

Casey crossed her arms over her chest. Oh, how it hurt to think of the way Zach walked away from their marriage after less than a year. "He is not a lowlife, and I'd appreciate your keeping your opinions about my husband to yourself."

Casey's annoyance increased with her defense. She owed him no loyalty. The fiery rage that passed boiling point the minute Stacey showed her the paper in the airport parking lot returned. The red heart-marked classified ad was a red flag to her already frayed nerves.

When Zach left, the almost unbearable stress compared to an out-of-control roller coaster. One minute, she sobbed in despair, her salty tears sufficient to form another ocean. And then the next, she raged like a wild woman. It was a miracle the kitchen cabinet doors still hung after the way she'd taken her anger out on them, wishing she could get her hands on Zachary Taylor just long enough to exercise the overwhelming hostility.

After the first week he was gone, Casey gave serious consideration to skipping the scheduled seminar. Upon realizing he wasn't coming back, she decided a change of scenery would probably do her good. Casey added a couple of vacation days and spent the second week in San Francisco.

Reconciling Zach's reasoning was impossible, simply because she had no idea why he left. How could he expect her to trust him to do the right thing for them both? Casey noted her hands were trembling and frowned. She had to calm down.

"You have no idea where he is or why he left. How long do you plan to brood over him?"

"As long as I want." Regret filled her at Stacey's sad smile. "I'm sorry," Casey said softly, touching her sister's arm. "You don't deserve that after all I've put you through."

"It was nothing," Stacey discounted, negotiating the narrow driveway and parking beside the guest house.

"Sure it was." Casey got out of the car and moved around the back of the car. "You let me move in with you when I thought I'd die if I stayed at the house. You put up with my multiple personalities. And no one else could have listened as you have."

Stacey pulled a suitcase from the trunk and headed for the house, calling over her shoulder, "Okay, so we agree I'm a great person. I'm still not going to find out who placed that ad."

Casey followed, drawing to a halt beside Stacey at the petti-coat table in the entryway. As they stood there, it occurred to her that the antique's purpose was completely lost on Stacey's black leather miniskirt. It could barely be seen in the mirrored bottom that ladies of old had used to check their hems. "Well, I didn't really want to know anyway."

"I'll bet."

Casey ignored her sarcasm. "It's great to be home."

"Only you would say that after a week in San Francisco," Stacey murmured, fingering a tendril of the dark hair hugging her skull as she primped in the mirror. "What gives? Why didn't you stay for your last day of vacation?"

"I needed to relax." And she would. Already she had formed a plan to incorporate some, maybe all, of her favorite things into her last vacation day. So far the list had infinite possibili-ties: definitely tea with her best friend, Emily, and she'd love to make a find for her parents' antique showroom, for, unlike Stacey, she knew the difference between Duncan Phyfe and Queen Anne.

They moved into the drawing room, Casey's eyes touching on every piece of furniture as she settled into her favorite bro-cade wing chair.

Stacey dropped down on the *Seignoret* sofa with much less aplomb than the valuable piece deserved. "Don't say it," she warned, kicking off her shoes and bringing her feet up onto the chair. "I get real tired of living in a showroom. I'd settle for one decent sofa."

"At least you didn't redecorate while I was gone. I kept envisioning this ultramodern decor and us homeless."

"There are other houses besides the one in our parents' backyard."

"True, but where else could we find such beautiful quarters

for free? Not to mention the privilege of viewing a half million dollars' worth of antiques daily."

"Privilege?" Stacey snorted her disdain. "We're doing them a favor. Who else would they trust with their precious antiques when they go off on their treasure-finding junkets?"

Casey shook her head in disbelief. "I find it incredibly difficult to believe you're the daughter of two highly respected antique dealers."

Lazily, Stacey's head rolled to the side, flashing her twin a knowing grin. "Maybe Mom and Dad can deny me, but you'd have problems."

"Can't you appreciate the beauty around you? The rugs? The furniture? The paintings? The collections? Doesn't it excite you to know we own a piece of history that was here before us and will remain long after we're gone?"

Stacey grabbed a small pillow and tucked it beneath her head. "Not particularly."

Casey released her long-suffering sigh. When would she learn? Years of effort on their parents' part hadn't resulted in Stacey's conversion to the family mold. Not everyone loved antiques. Definitely not Stacey, who had once shocked her parents by saying she'd lived with old all her life and wanted something new.

"What are we doing for dinner tonight?" Stacey asked.

"Let's order in. How about pizza?"

Stacey thrust her feet to the floor and sat up. "You want pizza?"

A slow grin crept over Casey's face as she nodded. She didn't understand the strange craving, but pizza had been in her thoughts ever since boarding her flight for home. "Make my half vegetarian. I'm going to change."

❧

Casey slid her heels off and bent to place them in the neatly aligned closet rack. One more day until she resumed her night shifts in the hospital nursery. She'd missed her babies, but as usual, she would have an all new batch to love upon her return. Unzipping her dress, she stepped out and slid the garment onto a hanger. Casey sorted through her suitcase for more casual clothes.

The newspaper caught her eye. She reached for it and reread the ad. *Slugger*. Casey tensed at Zach's pet name for her, her heart plummeting so quickly it almost rocked her. She shook her head as thoughts of his playful teasing took control, forcing her attention back to the words.

For a while, I forgot the importance of those words we spoke on our wedding day. Please give me a chance to explain.

Had he put the ad in the paper? Or did she want him to be responsible for the romantic gesture? Probably the latter, she thought glumly. During some of her more livid moments, she had decided on a future without Zach. Casey groaned at the thought of her mercurial behavior. She'd also told herself it was time to move on with her life but spent more time coming up with reasons why she didn't want other men.

Only Zachary Taylor. She wanted to know where he was. What he was doing. Why he'd left. And why he didn't love her as much as she loved him. Everything had been as perfect as life could get until she'd returned home to find him packed and ready to go.

The paper crumpled in her damp hands. Oh, whom did she think she was fooling? Looking at the situation through love-glazed eyes didn't make it better. If things had been so wonderful, Zach would be here now and they would be working out their problems.

Instead she slept alone, missing the man who had said he couldn't be her husband anymore. Did she still love him? Of course she did. And if wishful thinking could bring about a miracle, Zach had placed that ad. But Stacey was right. It didn't seem like a Zachary Taylor sort of act.

The doorbell chimed. *That couldn't be the pizza already,* she thought.

"Casey. It's for you."

Who could it be? Nobody knows I'm back yet. "Just a minute." Casey scrambled into a robe, tying the sash as she ran for the stairs. Downstairs, she drew to a halt by the open door, blinking furiously at the vision before her.

"Mrs. Bordeaux-Taylor?"

Casey managed a nod; she watched, stunned, as a man in a white bodysuit wearing a padded red heart about his middle sat his boom box on the floor. He depressed a button and began the performance of his life, lip-syncing to the song she recognized without effort. On the night he proposed, Zach insisted they have a song, and the beach music song suited them perfectly. Placing the ring on her finger, he sang about how he'd always love her. What a joke! Always barely lasted a year.

"Who sent you?" The words croaked out.

The man retrieved a heart-shaped note from a pocket within the padded suit. "He said to give you this."

Casey tore into the little red envelope, vaguely aware of the voices as she read the note.

Chuckling, Stacey closed the door after the messenger. "Wasn't he great? Maybe I'll use him sometime." She hesitated after one look at Casey's white face. "Zach?"

She nodded and passed Stacey the note.

" 'I tried to come home last week. Please let me explain,' " Stacey read aloud. "What does that mean?"

"Where is he?" Casey shrieked. A distinct ripping sound followed as she rammed her fists deep into the pockets of the robe.

"Have you tried the house?"

"It's not Zach," Casey denied, prowling the length of the entrance hall. "Just some practical joker."

The thought stopped her cold, bewilderment collecting in her throat as tears watered her view. He wouldn't do that to her. Theirs had been a special love. She'd always believed she and Zach were forever. But she'd been wrong about that, too.

❧

Time passed more quickly than Casey thought possible. She spent the last day of her vacation at an estate auction. After a second restless night, filled with both good and bad thoughts about the happenings since her arrival home, she left the house early to sit and think at Riverfront Park. When the tranquility of the Cape Fear River failed to restore her calm, she went to visit her best friend.

She'd known Emily Davies long before Emily had become Mrs. Franklin Benton. A newlywed herself, Emily had married the pastor only months before. The couple lived in the Davies' family home. Over tea in the widow's walk, they watched the river sparkle and caught up on the news.

"Pretty," Casey said when the jangle of Emily's bracelet caught her attention.

She held out her arm to show the gold bracelet with the Ten Commandments charms. "My three months' anniversary gift. I loved the bracelet right away but wasn't sure Franklin caught the hint."

Casey laughed and agreed. "Sometimes they don't hear those subtle suggestions."

"So tell me about your trip and what you've been doing."

When the conversation turned to the incidents since her return, Emily's what-ifs raised an even bigger question. What would Casey do if Zach wanted to come back?

"Have you prayed about this anger, Casey?" Emily asked.

"Everyone at church is praying for you and Zach."

Casey covered her face with one hand as tears filled her eyes. Pride made her want to cry out that nothing was wrong with their perfect marriage. "I tried. I asked God to send Zach home. He didn't. I get furious when I think about what Zach did."

"Don't be so tough on yourself," Emily said, plucking a tissue from the box on the end table and moving to Casey's side. "It hasn't been all that long. I'd be more worried if you *weren't* acting this way."

Casey dried her eyes. "I'm afraid. I feel like such a failure. I thought I knew Zach. How could this happen?"

"You always talked about the romance," Emily said. "I often wondered if you had time to deal with plans for the future before you married."

Casey frowned. "Of course we did. We discussed what we wanted out of life—careers, home, and family."

"Were you in agreement? Did Zach agree to you working? I know he doesn't like the same type of houses you do."

"We dealt with all that as the need arose. It was hard to arrange our schedules to have time together, but we worked it out. And his house was okay."

Emily took a sip of tea and set the cup back on the table. "You loved each other but were you friends? Do you trust him? What place did God have in your lives? Your plans?"

Casey moved over to the window, watching a barge push a big boat down the river. "We worshipped together. Church and Bible study when our schedules permitted."

"Did you pray together? Did God have a place in your home?"

Unable to answer to the affirmative, she turned to face her friend. "You and Franklin didn't date that long. Why are things different for you?"

"We were older, and from the beginning we courted with

marriage as the end result. He, being a minister, probably kept God in our romance."

Emily's questions opened up so many doubts for Casey. They were both Christians, but had they allowed God to lead their relationship? And while she loved Zach dearly, Casey admitted she didn't always understand him.

Like any woman in love, she had considered herself capable of changing him into the man she wanted him to be without nagging him to death. She would get past his tendency to be overprotective and teach him to open up and share. After all, they had a lifetime.

"Oh, I don't know, Emily. Right now, I feel like I'm married to a stranger. How could he hurt me this way?"

"Maybe you should find him and get it over with. Dreading a situation never helps."

"Not yet."

"Pray about this, Casey. Could be God's giving you a second chance."

Casey lingered too long and had to race home to dress in her uniform. The phone rang as she started out the door, and Casey hesitated long enough to make sure the answering machine was on. She wilted against the door frame when Zach spoke her name.

Though she hadn't heard the voice for days, it was a sound that would remain with her for the rest of her natural life. All the hurts resurfaced. Pride wouldn't allow her to forget the things he'd said. Zach couldn't expect to waltz back into her life and be forgiven. Not after failing to trust her to stand by him in whatever crisis had caused him to walk out of her life.

She pulled herself upright and ran out of the house. The car started easily. Casey threw it into gear, looking over her shoulder as she backed down the narrow driveway.

Maybe he didn't want to come back. Maybe he wanted a

divorce. Maybe he thought she hated him enough to sign separation papers without argument.

That was the real reason she couldn't talk to Zach. As long as she never heard the words, there was still hope for them. Casey groaned and chastised herself. "Oh, get a life, why don't you?"

Knowing Zach as she did, he probably wanted to talk about an amicable parting of the ways. Particularly since they had to work together. Well, she'd see about that. There was no way she could bear to see him every day.

Traffic slowed as Casey neared the hospital, and a new billboard caught her eye. At first she thought it was her imagination, but curiosity forced her to circle the block and drive by again.

Brilliant fuschia. Her favorite color.

I love you, Casey. Forgive me.

Casey couldn't get to the hospital staff parking lot fast enough. She slammed the door so hard it rocked the car. *Of all the nerve. He had to use my name. It wasn't enough that he left in the first place. No, he had to come back and make a public declaration. I'll be the laughingstock of the hospital.*

Well, the good doctor is going to find it isn't quite that easy. I'll find him if I have to look under every rock in the city, and when I do, he'll pay for playing me for a fool. I'll get to the bottom of this once and for all. Zachary Taylor has played enough games with my heart.

Her stride lengthened as she neared the staff lounge. Once inside, Casey dialed the office number from memory and got the answering service. *Desperate times call for desperate measures.* "I need to get an emergency message to Dr. Taylor."

"Who's calling please?"

"Mrs. Taylor."

"Mrs. Taylor, he instructed us to tell you he's at the hospital, room 313, when you called."

Casey thanked the woman and hung up. *When I called.* Zach was too certain of himself. Of her. She squared her shoulders and jerked the door open. She wasn't the same person he'd walked out on. Heartache had a way of forcing one to get to the nucleus of the matter, and it was time Zach understood this wasn't a game.

"Welcome back," Tricia called as Casey rounded the third floor nursing station. "How was the seminar?"

Casey smiled at her friend. "Great. The vacation days were even better. I'll fill you in later. I need to run by 313 before my shift."

"Wait a sec," Tricia said, the summons of a patient taking her attention. Casey waited, growing more impatient by the minute when another call followed.

There wasn't much time. Just enough to tell Zach it was time they talked. Her gaze drifted down the hallway where the room was located, hoping to catch him if he left the room before she got there.

Finally she tapped her watch and waved at Tricia, not slowing her pace in the hopes that she wouldn't lose her nerve.

"Casey, wait. He's. . ."

She missed the woman's doubt-filled expression as patient demands once again claimed Tricia's attention.

This hall has never seemed so long, Casey thought, her shoes silent on the carpeted floor. She pushed the door open and stared at the back of the man's head. The patient had thick, black curls. So like Zachary's. She shouldn't have come.

She took a step backward and drew to a halt. Something was wrong. Zach didn't treat adults. He was a pediatrician.

"Did you bring something for the pain?" the man requested, slowly turning his head toward the door. "Casey," Zach cried, the obvious delight edged with wariness. "I knew you'd come."

Zach. Traction. Hospital. Her mind assimilated the facts in bits and pieces.

"Casey?" he called anxiously when her skin paled even more. "Are you okay?"

There was no response as she jerked the door open and ran out, oblivious to his pleas. Casey leaned against the wall, sucking deep breaths to fight the black cloud that hovered over her as the strength drained from her body. He was back. Zachary Taylor was back.

"Casey?" Tricia called as she shook her arm. "Are you okay? I told Zach he shouldn't hide this from you." Casey recognized the woman didn't know who needed her worse. Zach's tumult sounded out into the hallway. "I've got to calm him down. He needs this shot."

The betrayal in Casey's eyes spoke loudly as she pushed herself straight. "Sorry I disturbed your patient."

"Casey, wait," Tricia called after her. "He needs you."

"He said he didn't," Casey whispered as she made a head-long dash for escape. Tears chased each other down her face as she raced madly down the hall. Zach had come home.

&

"Casey? Are you okay? Answer me!"

The pounding and yelling sounded muted in her fight to regain her control. Casey caught a glimpse of herself in the cheval mirror. What a sight. The once crisp uniform was a wrinkled mess, the redness of her eyes second only to the brilliance of a stop signal. Had the nursing director sensed the hysteria in her voice when she'd called in sick?

How could Zach not tell her he was in the hospital? Was it some sort of joke? Or a trick to get her to forgive him? He had plotted and connived, hoping to machinate her into seeing him, using what he knew of her nature to play on her sympathies. How else could he think she would react to his deceit?

"Casey, don't lock yourself away," Stacey called. "Talk to me. Zach said he's sorry."

The door slammed against the wall with a sudden impetus, and the Casey who stood there was far from her normal, sweet-natured self. "How could he?" she demanded.

Anxiety filled Stacey's expression and Casey understood she felt her pain as her own. "Maybe it's for the best. You've been miserable without him."

Casey hated losing control, and that was exactly what was happening. She was so angry. It wasn't her nature to hurt others, but she wanted to strike out now. She wanted to hurt Zach as badly as he had hurt her. "I've been miserable because of him."

"Would you rather be wretched with or without him? If it's without, I'll be happy to tell him to take a hike. Just as soon as he can walk. If he walks. He claims he just wants to tell you what happened."

Terror controlled Casey's heartbeat. Lightheaded, her eyes drifted shut. Slowly, she opened them, relieved to find everything normal. "What do you mean 'if'? Has my husband made you his confidant too?"

"No!" Stacey cried, clasping Casey's hands in hers. "He told me about the accident and the therapy he'll need to get back on his feet. Nothing else. I don't want to know why Zach left, but I figured you did."

It was true. More than anything else, Casey wanted to know how he could hold her in his arms and declare undying love in the morning and then say it was all over that afternoon.

"How long have you known?" Casey asked suspiciously.

"Right after you left his room. Zach called the office. He's concerned he may have pushed you too far."

"Funny time to be concerned."

Stacey nodded. "He asked if I'd heard from you. I gave

him some real attitude. He told me he was in the hospital. I felt pretty bad after he agreed that he deserved that treatment. He said he loved you and asked how he could get you to talk to him. Zach said he was pretty out of it for the first week. He transferred here Monday."

"Tricia didn't even tell me. She just let me walk in without a word."

"She called a few minutes ago. Said she was sorry. She found it difficult not to help him play Cupid when she knows how right you two are for each other."

Casey rubbed her hands over her face. "I can't believe he didn't tell me he was in the hospital. In traction."

"You were out of town," Stacey reminded.

"You had the number. What happened?"

"Car accident. He skidded into a bridge railing. The vehicle's a total loss."

Her legs felt like old rubber bands left in the sun until the elasticity melted away. Casey sank to the floor, more shaken than she cared to admit as her mind registered the significance of the words.

Stacey sat beside her and took her hand. "What are you going to do?"

"Do his parents know?"

"He asked them not to come. Said you were here and he didn't want them coming from Vegas."

"He'd better call his mom. I'm sure he'd like the company. Zach never was much for spending time alone."

"You mean you're not going to—"

Casey looked Stacey straight in the eye. "I don't know what I'll do."

"Don't make it something you'll regret."

"I did that when I married Zachary Taylor." At her sister's startled look, Casey quickly retracted the words. "I didn't mean it." Her voice trembled with the emotion that washed over her in waves.

Stacey drew her into her arms. "I know you didn't. Will you at least see him?"

"I can't say right now."

"Aren't you even curious, Casey? Isn't it worth taking a chance to learn why he left?"

"I'm not the risk taker, sister dear. I leave that area in your capable hands. I need to lie down. I don't feel well."

※

He turned his head to the door that opened onto the semi-darkened room, the wall light casting a shadow over the bed.

"Zach?"

"Casey?" His head lifted, the smile lighting his features momentarily before it faded. "Oh, it's you."

"Good to see you, too, Zach. At least you're still awake."

"Who said I was?"

"Fine," Stacey snapped, whirling toward the door. "I just stopped by to tell you Casey's okay. Maybe I'll call tomorrow. After you lose the attitude."

"Wait," Zach called frantically. "You don't know what it's like. Hanging in the air, forced to endure bed pans, never seeing anyone."

"I'm here now."

"And I appreciate your visit. I just wish Casey. . ." Uneasiness clouded his face. He shouldn't have tricked Casey, but thanks to his foolishness there wasn't much hope he could stride back into their home and confront her with the truth. "I know she's angry," he offered tiredly. "I tried to call a few minutes ago. She doesn't answer."

"Zach, you have to be patient."

"I am a patient, Stacey. How long do you think I can wait? She's my wife. I love her."

"And you're going to have a difficult time convincing her of that."

"I was confused."

"She was worried sick, and you didn't even call."

His gaze dropped from her face, his tone contrite as he said, "I was coming home when the accident happened."

"Was it necessary to do so much damage?"

"I wasn't thinking. I lost control."

"I'd say that happened before you left," Stacey murmured. "I don't want to hear this. She already thinks I'm in your confidence. Just remember, Casey is not the world's easiest woman to convince."

"I know. I owe Casey the truth. I just hope she accepts what I have to tell her."

"You'd better not hurt her again, Zach. Casey just reminded me she wasn't a risk taker, but I figure she must have been to marry you."

"You're going to help me?"

"You bet, brother-in-law. You're the only thing, other than antiques, that I've ever seen light my sister's eyes. For some reason, I always figured she'd go after a crusty old antique dealer. I suppose she still could. Though from the way she jumps to your defense, I doubt she will."

He moved suddenly. "You mean. . .?" Zach stilled as his actions brought pain.

"You idiot. How are you going to get better when you do stupid things like that? Should I call the nurse?"

"Didn't they warn you not to overexcite me?"

"I am not the problem here, Zach."

"Tell me what Casey said," he demanded.

"I called you a lowlife."

An indignant frown marred the handsome face. "You're a real pal, Stace. What next? If you were considering stringing me up, I'm halfway there."

The smile turned the corners of her mouth upward, and Zach felt pain like a dull scalpel twisting in his gut as he looked upon the wrong half of a matched set. Although he'd never admit it to Casey and Stacey, their almost indistinguishable appearances amazed and sometimes confused him.

Mirror reflections from the top of their heads to the bottoms of their size four shoes, Casey and Stacey shared hair so black it had a blue sheen, doe-brown eyes, petite five-foot frames, and what his wife sarcastically referred to as terminal cuteness.

Inside and out, Casey was the most beautiful woman he'd ever known. If only he could go back in time to that last happy morning. He missed his wife.

"How are you going to get her to talk to you?"

"I could call in a favor, get her transferred to this floor," he suggested.

"Trust her angel-of-mercy instincts that much, do you?"

"You're right. I need to gain her sympathy before trying that one. And then, there's always the truth."

"A novel approach," Stacey muttered. "I just hope that doesn't blow up in your face."

❧

So Stacey had gone to the hospital. Casey replaced the phone. She called the Nursing Director to apologize for her behavior. The woman had been very sympathetic, saying she understood and hoped Casey found Dr. Taylor improved when she visited him last night.

She'd give her busybody sister a piece of her mind the moment she laid eyes on her again. Oh, why waste her breath? Stacey never listened. Even as kids, Stacey never gave a single thought to the consequences of anything she did. Their parents frequently called them double trouble, but the truth was Stacey was one twin pulling double duty.

Stacey managed to get them both into more scrapes than Casey cared to count. And being five minutes, well, actually one day, older since they had been born at 11:57 P.M. and 12:02 A.M. on separate days in separate months, always seemed to make Casey the wiser when it came to their parents' reprimands.

After a brief rap, Stacey's head popped around the edge of the door. "I went to see Zach. He's in pretty bad condition."

Casey's brows lifted. "Why, Stacey?"

"He's family. What's going on? I've never known you to act this way."

Casey had never been as angry or hurt. A scream of frustration clawed at her throat and she blurted, "Stop butting into my life. We're not kids anymore."

"Fine," Stacey huffed, turning her back and marching toward the doorway. "That's the last favor I plan to do for you."

"Great. Wonderful. I can only hope," Casey shouted as a bedroom door slammed down the hall.

❧

"Hello, Zach, it's me."

"Stacey? What's wrong? Has Casey. . .? Is she. . .?"

"She's upset with me."

"What did she say? Tell me," he demanded impatiently.

"Don't yell at me," she snapped. "I'm sick of being used as a whipping boy by you two."

He let out a long, audible breath. "I'm sorry. Please tell me what she said."

"She's confused. Hurt. Angry. Seeing you like this has really upset her."

"I knew I should have told her what happened. I just went overboard when that child—"

"Zach, stop. Casey's the one you need to tell."

"I know. Casey isn't going to like my next move."

"I don't want to know, Zach."

"You already do."

two

"Why me?" Casey asked, a cynical inner voice cutting through the Nursing Supervisor's words and insisting she already knew the answer.

"You're the only nurse I have who can handle the floor."

"And that's the only reason?"

Pat Stone looked Casey in the eye and asked, "What other reason could I have?"

Casey shrugged. "Do I report immediately?"

"Please. I'll let them know in the nursery."

Praying she had not judged the woman unfairly, Casey left the office and moved toward the elevators. Maybe it was coincidental, but she found it difficult to believe Zach wasn't involved. Not when on the day after learning her husband was in the hospital, she received a reassignment to his floor. Maybe the smart thing would be to meet this thing head on, but she couldn't. Not yet. No matter how much she loved him.

And no matter how hard Zach pushed, he would not rush her. One thing she'd learned as a head nurse was to delegate. She'd see Zach when she was ready and not one second before.

❧

"This is getting ridiculous," the aid grumbled when the signal for room 313 flashed on. "I'm sorry, but I just can't deal with him again. We've tried everything short of sedation."

"Now, there's a thought." Casey flipped the switch. "Yes, Dr. Taylor?"

"The aid hasn't brought my water pitcher back and. . ."

Pity Zach hadn't broken his fingers as well, Casey thought, listening to yet another complaint. They were too short-staffed to handle such a demanding patient. She would request a special duty nurse tomorrow. "Someone will be there shortly, sir."

The aid looked almost frantic when Casey turned around. She patted the woman's shoulder. "Relax. I'm going."

In the kitchenette, Casey forced herself to remain calm as she scooped ice into the container and added water. For good measure, she picked up Zach's nighttime snack. She refused to fetch and carry all night.

At his door, she tapped and pushed it open. "Here I am, Zach. Hasn't that been the purpose of the manipulation and aggravation?"

The black brows drew downward in a frown. "Casey, I just want. . ."

"You're a spoiled brat, Zachary Taylor." Seething as she arranged the items on the bedside tray with more than necessary force, she added, "And I say that as a nurse on a floor where there are several sick patients with whose care you, a doctor, are interfering."

"Why not say it as my wife?"

"Because I'm not certain I want to be your wife." There it was, the hurt, little boy expression he did so well. It wasn't going to work this time. "Don't push me, Zach."

"Don't you want to hear the story?"

"Did you give me the option before? Or are you so bored with being flat on your back you figure it's a good way to pass the time? No, wait," she said as he started to speak. "I'm angry. Very much so. That's why I haven't come in here before. Angry because you left. Angry because you conspired with my friends. Just angry for the principle of it, and this isn't helping matters.

"Because now you're interfering with my work." Casey

filled his water cup, replaced the straw, and set it within easy reach. "There's your water. You know as well as I do that the traction is set up as ordered. If it's uncomfortable, I'll be happy to call your doctor. If you're in pain and need stronger medication, I'll call the doctor. But these constant calls to the nurses' station have to stop. Maybe you never heard the story about the little boy who cried wolf."

His blue gaze fixed on her. "You wouldn't."

Her stubborn expression was at odds with his words. "If you persist, I'll recommend a private duty nurse effective immediately. My staff does not have time to pander to you."

"That's it, Casey. Let him know who's boss."

Two pairs of startled eyes focused on their friend and Zach's physician, David Burns.

"Hello, Zachary. What are you doing now?"

"Trying to talk to my wife."

"I'm not your wife here. If what I suspect is true, I'm on this floor because you pulled some strings. I'm trying to do my job, and you're being a highly disruptive patient." She turned to the doctor. "Tell him to stop with the call button. I don't have one staff member left who's willing to deal with his constant demands. Either that or get him a private duty nurse."

Casey was out the door in a flash, her heart pounding. Even when they were acquainted personally and professionally, nurses did not issue ultimatums to doctors. Anyone with a grain of sense knew that. But then she wasn't just a nurse. She had a personal stake in this, and she was very tired of Zach's childish games. She'd do everything possible in her duties as a nurse to aid in his recovery, but she wouldn't be harassed.

૨૦

"You're pushing too hard."

"You tell me what I should do, David. You've got me hanging here like a side of beef. I can't pursue her. If I don't keep trying, she might never give me a chance to explain," Zach said in a voice edged with terror. It had taken him very little time to realize he didn't want to lose Casey. He'd been only partially alive without her.

"Maybe not, but it's her choice. I take it you plan to resume your practice?" At Zach's affirmative response, he suggested, "Knock it off with the nursing staff. Being the fair-haired boy was always important to you. Ticking off the staff could hurt the image."

"I want the attention of only one."

David scribbled on the chart and glanced up. "I've been trying to figure out how Casey got assigned to this floor. Is she right? Was it your doing?"

Zach pushed back the guilt. Sure, he'd considered pulling a few strings, but he was innocent. There had been no need to carry his plan through. "Ask the Nursing Director."

"I'd rather ask Tricia Simpson's sick father," David murmured, the thick gray-black brows raised in question.

"How is Tricia's dad?"

"You mean it's not a setup?" David questioned.

"I had nothing to do with the assignment. I was as surprised as everyone else to learn Casey was working on this floor. You didn't answer my question. How am I supposed to get her to listen to what I have to say?"

"Stop pushing so hard, Zach. Give her time to come to grips with her emotions. Now, what's this in your chart about you being uncomfortable?"

❧

Casey preferred to use the lull in late night activity to catch up on paperwork, but the charts lay untouched as her thoughts drifted to the patient in room 313. Could she handle whatever God had in store for them this time?

How well she remembered the part destiny had played in

their initial meeting. Had it only been little more than a year ago that Zach had come to the house to pick Stacey up for a blind date? He acknowledged her lack of welcome with an immediate response of "You're disappointed."

Casey hadn't a clue as to why he would think that, but her reaction to him had not been disappointment.

"I'm Zachary Taylor. Dee showed me your picture so I would recognize you."

She almost laughed in his face. "I take it Dee didn't show you a family shot." At his confused look, she murmured, "Just a minute."

The shock blended with understanding once she showed him her parents' favorite photograph of their daughters. He did a double take, his gaze shifting from the picture to her and back, almost as if he couldn't believe there were two of them. "Identical twins?"

"Scary, huh?" Casey teased, inviting him in. "I'm Casey. I'm sure Stacey will be here shortly."

She kept Zach company until Stacey called to say she was stuck at the office. When he suggested she join him for dinner, Casey agreed.

It took her only a few hours to realize she liked him more than any other man she'd ever met. For the first time in her life, she'd done something totally out of character and stolen another woman's man. Well, not actually stolen, but by the time Zach got around to meeting her sister, Casey knew which twin he preferred.

She insisted Stacey wouldn't really care for Zachary Taylor, claiming he was too intellectual, too involved in medicine—anything she could think of to convince her sister he wasn't her type.

Other dates followed and the quickness of their developing relationship shocked them both. Zach was a romantic, sweeping her off her feet with his extravagant courtship. Every date was a well-planned and executed adventure. They never fought over what they would do, and he always made the plans.

Though they had very little in common, Casey refused to allow that to stand in her way. Not even the few years' age difference mattered. She felt blessed to find such a wonderful Christian man.

Casey loved everything about him. Zachary Taylor was a beautiful sight, a handsome compact man who walked with a spring in his step. The way he talked, his soft, reassuring physician's voice, mesmerized her. His eyes, a shocking brilliant blue—glowed every bit as brightly as a neon sign—were spellbinding and absolutely beautiful. Her one hope for their children was that they have Zachary Taylor's eyes. So much more riveting than her own doe brown. Those eyes and his lustrous black curls.

When Zach proposed, she immediately said yes, confident he was the man God intended for her. Now she realized it wasn't because they had sought God's guidance. Their wedding was a small affair, mostly family with a few friends. Casey remembered her nervousness coupled with finely edged excitement and how quickly the doubts were overcome by her desire to become Mrs. Zachary Taylor.

She wore her mother's heirloom gown and caught her breath with pleasure at the sight of Zach in his black tails when she descended the wide staircase of her parents' home.

The reception had been held in the ballroom. They slipped away to share a few kisses, and it hadn't been long before he'd whisked her away to their honeymoon haven, Solitude.

She hadn't given up her job, and from the beginning their biggest conflict was coordinating their schedules. It hadn't taken Casey long to learn Zachary Taylor was the most overprotective man who ever walked the earth. He took his role as head of the home very seriously, and to him, burdens were for his shoulders only.

When she wanted to discuss their work, Zach listened but always put her off when she asked about his. After a while, she decided to enjoy the parts he shared and wait for the others.

Casey was certain he considered seeing her now only because he was sure of full recovery. Otherwise, she'd never have known.

Their lovemaking was wonderful. A considerate lover, Zach always made certain she was as fulfilled as he was. Never once had she ever regretted loving him. Not even after their last time together. That morning had been the glue that held Casey together, her certainty that no man could have loved as he had and suddenly stop caring. Love too grand to have just disappeared.

"It certainly has gotten quieter around here," Sue said as she came around the nurses' station.

The pencil rolled from Casey's nerveless fingers. "Almost time for the next shift."

"What did you say to Dr. Taylor?"

"I told the good doctor a few home truths about his selfishness and said I'd request a private duty nurse if he didn't knock it off."

"Is it what I think?"

Casey shrugged. "I suppose so."

"We hated to send you. Figured you. . . Well, I know how I'd feel."

That was the most difficult part for Casey. Everyone knew the story, or at least the gossip. She'd been horrified by some of the speculation that had drifted back to her, wondering time and time again how Zach could have done this to her, too ashamed to admit she didn't know the true story either.

"Don't they say doctors always make the worst patients?"

she managed, hoping the response was as nonchalant as she intended. "Don't worry about me. I'm in charge of dealing with the difficult patients. This just happens to be personal."

"I wasn't trying—"

"I know," Casey said, laying a hand on the woman's arm. "Zach and I will work this out. Until then, you'll have to bear with us both."

৯

"And then Zach called again." Casey perched on the side of Stacey's bed. "That made at least a dozen times. I couldn't believe he'd be so inconsiderate."

"He's trying to get your attention."

"Believe me, he has. I never realized he could be so selfish. Maybe love is blind."

"He's a man with a cause."

"I don't like being manipulated. First, it was forcing me to see him. Then it was getting me assigned to that floor. I know he's responsible. Don't ask how. I just know. He tried the same thing with the call button. Honestly, Stacey, all I want is time to work this out, but Zach wants what he wants."

"You."

"He had me. And zap, he's gone, telling me it's for the best. I'm a bit tired of his one-sided reasoning. Oh, enough of this," she declared with a weary shake of her head. "I've had all I can deal with today. I need a hot bath and bed. By the way, have you seen my new antiques magazine?" Casey laughed at Stacey's grimace. "You should try it sometime."

"Why don't you go into the business with Mom and Dad?"

"They have so much fun together. If I worked with them, they'd feel obligated to send me on some of their buying trips, maybe even insist I accompany them. They deserve this time alone together." An easy smile played at the corners of Casey's mouth when she added, "Besides, I like nursing for now, and when they decide to retire, I'll be ready to take over."

"So nursing's not forever?"

"Never has been. It just seemed like a good field for me. I always was the compassionate one."

"Oh yeah, sure," Stacey said, flinging a decorative pillow at her sister's departing back.

❧

"Hi, Stacey. Is she there?"

"In the tub with the latest antiques magazine."

"Her two loves," came Zach's rueful reply. "Any comments about me?"

"You're ticking her off."

"No joke. She'd have strangled me last night if my doctor hadn't walked in, but at least I stir some emotion in her."

"The wrong one, Zachary dear. I know my sister, and when she gets angry, she tends to eliminate the problem."

"What's she going to do with me?"

"Last I heard, she's working on this incredible plan involving a couple of interns and a big window. I told her a runaway patient bed on a level floor wouldn't work. If I were you, I wouldn't let them roll me near any inclines."

"I don't suppose she'd talk to me?"

"You mean after twelve hours of listening to you whine steadily? I doubt it. Oh, and by the way, she's on to you getting her transferred to your floor."

"Hey, I'm innocent," Zach declared. "I didn't do anything. Tricia Simpson's father really had a heart attack."

"Good grief," Stacey uttered. "Is he all right?"

"I haven't heard."

"I'd better tell Casey. They're friends."

"You'll work on her, won't you, Stacey?"

"Afraid not. She told me to butt out. You're on your own from here on out."

"You can't abandon me now. I need your help. She wouldn't listen. I can't even get her to stay in the same room with me for more than two minutes."

Stacey's heavy sigh echoed over the phone.

"I was afraid of that," she said. "Oh, all right. Just try not to undo my efforts with any more of your brainstorms."

"You have to accept part of the responsibility. If you'd been at home that first night, you and I might be married."

"And I could be angry with you instead?"

"But more forgiving," he suggested.

"Guess again, buddy. Lucky for you, Casey's the twin with the forgiving nature."

"If you say so."

"It's the only reason I believe you've got a chance of convincing Casey you still love her. Bye, Zach. I won't tell her you called."

&

"I hate to say it, Casey, but your husband is becoming a pain. His newest tactic is calling out to the other patients' visitors when they come into the hall. He asks them to come talk to him and then sends them to get a nurse. They think we're ignoring him."

Casey listened to the Nursing Director describe the nightmare her life had become over the last few days. The entire hospital was abuzz with Zach's behavior, certain something was seriously wrong with Dr. Taylor. Personally, Casey attributed it to his being spoiled rotten by everyone in his life, including herself. "And what am I supposed to do?"

"Talk to him. The situation has become unbearable. Nobody wants to deal with Dr. Taylor."

That goes double for me, she thought. "I don't think I can make a difference."

"Do it as a nurse concerned for a patient. His recovery will take even longer if his attitude doesn't improve."

Casey leaned forward in the chair. "I've tried to forget he's my husband, to look at this from a professional viewpoint, but every time I so much as step into the room, he sees it as a potential opportunity to—"

"I do understand, Casey," the woman interrupted, "and we don't want to push you, but we feel you're the only one who can solve the problem."

Casey dragged her feet on the walk back to her floor. It appeared Zach was going to win after all. His stunts would force her to take action. She'd hoped to find peace after returning to the nursery, but her pleasure in caring for the newborns took second place to the questions nagging at her day and night.

Everyone believed she could help. She couldn't. The week at his beck and call hadn't helped. None of her arguments had gotten through his determined pursuit. He'd even started the gifts.

Zach courted her in the same way: flowers, candy, and then after a suitable period, the valuable stuff. In the past it had been jewelry and furniture, but he had gone for the big guns this time.

He'd truly hooked her with the lamp. Zach knew exactly how much she wanted one. She'd dragged him to enough estate auctions with no luck. She could hardly believe his success, and didn't even want to guess what he had paid for the exquisite Tiffany. But he did know her tastes, and each gift was something so desired it made it impossible to refuse.

This was the old Zach, the attentive, romantic lover who would apparently use anything to wheedle himself back into her good graces. Casey felt torn, tempted but unforgiving, a mental wreck. Something had to give soon, and it would probably be her mind. *Would Zach still want me after the nervous breakdown?* Casey wondered, suppressing a giggle as she barreled into David Burns.

"Hello, sir."

There was a strangely hopeful look on the man's face. "You weren't visiting Zach by any chance?"

"What is this? An all-out assault?" Casey demanded.

David shook his head and touched her arm. "Can we talk?"

Casey followed him into a vacant room along the hall. He gestured her into the chair and sat on the bed. "You know Zach's a diabetic?"

She did. It had been the one thing about her healthy, energetic husband that had come as a total surprise. He'd insisted they discuss his type I diabetes before becoming engaged. As a nurse she knew the basics, daily insulin injections, carefully regulated diet and exercise, but there was nothing textbook about life with a diabetic.

Learning to interpret moods had been important with his high stress job. His work made it even harder to keep him on a schedule. High blood sugar left Zach tired and depressed, low blood sugar brought anger and anxiety.

"We haven't been able to control his blood sugar with diet. I suspect it's related to lack of exercise and mental distress. If all goes well, we'll have him in therapy within a day or so."

"He'll be up and about that soon?"

"It's not that simple. The physical therapy will be extensive and exhaustive, and frankly, I'm concerned about his general attitude. I've had numerous complaints about my bad-boy patient. He's putting everyone off, and you know the reason as well as I."

"What would you have me do?" The outcry unleashed her indignation. "Forget the past; turn myself over to his whims?"

"You have to handle the situation however you see fit, Casey. I hoped you were closer to reconciliation. I'm concerned he's going to get depressed if things don't change soon. Zach has a long, difficult road ahead of him. Right now, he's fighting for your attention, but if he gives up, we both know what can happen."

As their eyes met, Casey felt shock run through her.

These people were expressing concern for the man she'd claimed to love with all her heart. What was she doing? Certainly not praying that God would help her say the right words, not asking Him to guide her actions. She was pouting, playing a convincing role as wronged wife. But what about Zach? What about his side of the story? What about this awful thing that had happened to him? She wasn't behaving like the Christian she claimed to be—not adhering to the wedding vows she'd spoken.

"I'll talk to him." Casey spoke softly, adding, "I'll see if I can convince him to devote his energy to getting better. That's all I can promise."

"It's a start."

It was difficult to shake the mood, but Casey had long ago learned that people in the medical profession dealt with the situation or got out. She'd learned to deal. It was time to take the babies to their mothers; afterward she could visit Zach. Just to talk.

"How's it going?" she asked Tricia minutes later.

"Not so good. He yelled at the last nurse. Claimed a monkey could give a better shot."

"Real prince, huh?"

"All the girls used to think so. Dr. Taylor was everyone's dream."

"Now he's their worst nightmare?"

Tricia nodded slowly. "We'll have to give awards for tolerating him."

"Don't hold it against him. He's not himself."

"Tell me about it."

"I'll tell him. Send security if you hear anything break."

"Believe me, there's nothing but plastic in that room."

Casey's insides did loop-de-loops as she walked down the hall. Just thinking of seeing him had her trembling. The old magnetism was powerful. The thing she'd fantasized most about, other than having him home, was being in his arms again.

Some nights she'd found herself awake, certain he was there with her. She tried to believe time would make a difference, but she knew that whether they were separated for one day or fifty years, her love for Zach would always be there.

She was angry with him. Was she trying to punish him for hurting her? If only things weren't so confused. *Lord, please help us through this,* Casey prayed silently as she watched Zach through the partially open door. His pain and exhaustion from fighting the equipment was evident in the way he lay, dejected, staring out the window.

She pushed the door open. "Hello, Zach."

His head jerked with the movement as he swung toward her, the blue eyes both questioning and glowing with excitement. "Casey."

She forced herself to calm down as she slid into the visitor's chair. "Still giving the staff a hard time, I hear. I've never known you to behave this way."

"I don't mean to be such a pain," he said, his voice dropping. "I hurt."

Casey was at his side in a flash. "Where?" It wasn't necessary that he be in pain.

"Here," he said, guiding her hand to his heart and then his stomach and to his head.

"Were you injured in those areas?"

"It's misery, Casey. I'm so unhappy and there's not a thing I can do."

Despite her fears, she felt some relief in learning she wasn't suffering alone. Maybe things weren't as bleak as she'd feared. "Stop feeling sorry for yourself," she said, pulling her hand from his. "What does the doctor say?"

"Therapy soon and then home. Will you come with me?"

"No."

Crestfallen, his smile quickly faded. "Why not, Casey? I'll need a nurse."

"It's not fair to me," she responded sharply, abandoning all pretense. "You know what happened—"

"Was wrong."

"Zach." She had to conquer her reaction to that pleading look of his.

"I ran away. I said and did a lot of stupid things. I was so mixed up, I couldn't think straight."

"Didn't you love me at all?"

"Yes, I loved. . .*love,* you. Won't you give me a chance to prove it, to regain your trust? To explain?"

Casey pulled her heart back behind the protective wall. "Zach, I don't think now is the time to discuss this."

"Come home with me, Casey." His tone was soft but desperate.

"To our house?"

"To the lake."

"No." Casey turned to stare out the window as the flashback scenes rolled in her head. How could he suggest they return to the place where they had both been the happiest? "Why do this to me, Zach? I came to talk about you and the hospital. You always enjoyed the respect of your colleagues and coworkers. I assume you plan to stay."

"Forever."

"Then it's time you accept responsibility for your attitude and your health. These people want the man they know and love."

"What do you want?"

"I'd like to see the old Zach. The one I know cares about other people." Casey glanced at her watch. "I've got to run. Think about what I said."

He loves me. That thought seemed to repeat itself with every step. *He loves me. He wants me to come home with him.* She wanted to go. But how was she to live with the past? She couldn't just forget, no matter how desperately she wanted to return to the morning before her world had fallen apart.

◆

Zach watched Casey leave, his hopes at having reached her even a little bit diminished by his thoughts. How would she react to knowing the truth about why he left? Was their love strong enough to confront what he must share with her? He didn't want to hurt her, but he seemed incapable of stopping. *It might have been better for all concerned if I had just died in the car accident.*

three

Casey let herself into the house, her thoughts on a conversation with Tricia before leaving the hospital. The woman praised Zach to the skies, saying how impressed she was by the way he was handling his pain. What had happened to the monster from room 313? Surely he hadn't changed so much in the past week.

Then again, maybe he had. Everywhere she went, it was Dr. Taylor this, Dr. Taylor that. All the staff kept telling her what a wonderful patient he was and how they just loved him. *If another person tells me how hard he is working on his therapy, I'll scream.* It seemed everyone had forgotten and forgiven. Their sympathies were all for him.

She found Stacey in the kitchen, eating breakfast. "Bad night?" she asked, her eyes probing Casey's face.

Offering a distracted nod, Casey returned her smile. "Honestly, Stacey, you should see the looks I get. Like I'm some sort of three-headed monster."

"Zach cleaned up his act that much, huh?"

"It's amazing." Casey took a bottle of apple juice from the refrigerator, twisted the top off, and walked over to pull out a chair. "The wonder doctor can do no wrong. I'm the villain."

"Maybe you should take time off and be his private duty nurse. You wouldn't have to endure the criticism."

"The looks are easier than those little meetings with Zach. I don't know that I can handle an overdose of those pleas he keeps throwing my way. Besides, he wants to go to Solitude. He knows I loved the time we spent there."

"Why don't you let him explain?"

"Because I'm afraid his excuses will be too simple. What if he ran away because of something we could have worked out by communicating?" Casey threw her hands up into the air. "Am I wrong to want to work this thing out in my head?"

"No. Zach's just impatient to have everything back the way it was. If he could wipe the time off the calendar, he would."

"Why won't he accept that he can't?"

"From what you've told me about him, he never was one to do things in a small way. You said yourself he could never accept half-measures."

"I believed that once. Before he left." Casey's voice broke.

"And you can't understand his half-measures now? You still don't have a clue as to what happened?"

"No," Casey said shortly as she set the juice bottle on the table with a thud and stood. "You'd better get dressed for work. I'm going to bed."

"What about your breakfast?"

"I'm not hungry."

"Don't let yourself get run down, Casey. It won't make things any easier."

"I know. See you in the morning."

She wasn't being fair to Stacey. Her sister had stood by her, comforting, listening, and struggling to keep her opinion to herself. At first, she couldn't understand that Casey didn't know why Zach left. But as they rehashed the events preceding that fateful day, she began to understand Casey's dilemma.

As she reached for her zipper, Casey thought about that afternoon all those weeks ago. She'd never forget. It was engraved into her conscious memory for all time. Maybe you never forget having your heart shattered.

Everything had seemed so normal. She came in from the

night shift and went directly to their bedroom, kissed Zach hello, and he'd kissed her back.

"You should see this newborn in the nursery," she chattered as she turned her back for him to undo her uniform zipper. "Black hair, blue eyes. I bet our baby would look exactly like him. Any thoughts on when we should start our family, Zach?" She had looked over her shoulder at him. Intense love flared in his eyes as he drew her down on the bed.

"I'm willing to work on it any time you want," he whispered. His lips claimed hers. The next few minutes were spent in a very intimate planning strategy. Later they rushed around, getting him out of the house before she went to bed.

That afternoon she left to run errands and came home to find him packing. His tone warned her something was seriously wrong as Casey sensed Zach's agitation, the underlying anger. "What is it? What's wrong?"

Why can't he look at me? she wondered as he averted his gaze, studying the carpeted flooring with alien intensity.

"I have to get out of your life. I can't risk your happiness. Just trust me to know what's right." The words poured from his mouth as he jammed clothes into the suitcase.

"Trust you?" Casey asked uncertainly. "You tell me you made a decision that affects both of us and expect me to trust your judgment? What happened? Zach, talk to me."

"If I thought it would work, I'd lie and say I don't love you. Anything to make you hate me enough to get you through."

She sat back, momentarily rebuffed as the words registered in her dizzied mind. Zach started to reach for her, but dropped the consoling hand to his side. "We're married. Any decisions are supposed to be mutual," she reasoned.

His response to her reasoning was to pick up his suitcase.

"If you love me so much, tell me what's going on." Even as she shouted the words at him, Casey tried to think of the possibilities. "What, Zach? Is it trouble at work? The hospital? Financial? Legal? Tell me. I'll stand by you. I love you too."

He glanced over his shoulder. "I can't. Believe it or not, one day you'll thank me for leaving."

Confusion warred with anger. Casey was scared witless by this stranger. This was not the man who vowed to love her forever—the man who, until this very moment, had proclaimed that undying love at every possible opportunity. He was an impostor. He might look like him, but this wasn't her Zach.

As if some force were shoving at her back, Casey trailed after him, choking back the sobs as she demanded, "Why won't you talk to me?" She grabbed a handful of shirt, fear giving her untold strength.

"Because if I let you talk me out of this, it'll destroy your life," he said, a stubborn, closed expression changing his handsome face.

Fury choked Casey. "Stop being so melodramatic."

"I'm not. I've let you reason me into believing many things during our marriage."

"Only because you wanted to. You're smart enough to know nothing's that bad."

"No, Casey. This time is different. You're not changing my mind."

"What about this morning?" came her anguished cry. "Why did you say we could start a family then, and now you're leaving?" His stoic expression and refusal to respond had Casey reeling like a crack to the jawbone. "Don't do this, Zach."

"I have to. Get on with your life. And let me get on with mine. I'll have my lawyer send over the papers."

"What papers?" The click of the door closing behind him was as loud as a bomb as it snapped shut. She grabbed the knob and wrenched it open. "If you leave without telling me what's going on, I'll never speak to you again."

"Good-bye, Casey."

"Zach, please!" she cried one last time as he walked out of her life.

And that had been the last Casey had heard from him until he showed up in the hospital.

Nothing made sense. They hadn't fought. A talk with his partner had left her just as confused. Donald had told her about Zach's brief insulin reaction the previous week at work. There was nothing spectacular in that, the situation easily reversed when he'd worked out his insulin/blood sugar balance.

At the hospital Casey heard about his losing a young patient that day and wondered if it had something to do with his strange behavior. But that didn't make sense either.

Zach had no bond with the dead child. The boy had been brought in that afternoon in a coma, beyond hope. From all accounts, Zach worked zealously to save his life.

Now he was back. Ready to explain why he walked out. Casey sighed. Maybe even to begin their life again. Perhaps it was time she listened.

ஜ

"You've got to do this, Stacey," Casey said, pacing restlessly across the room. "You promised."

"I said I'd tell him it was over if you wanted. I never said I'd pretend to be you. It wouldn't work."

"We've fooled others."

"Mom and Dad for a few minutes, a teacher now and then, our friends on occasion. Zach would see the difference right away. You're his wife."

"It's not fair, Stacey. If I go, I won't be able to refuse. You're tougher."

"I'm not that tough. I don't really understand why you have to say no. He's not saying the same bed, just the same house."

"With Zach, that's too close."

"You love him. Why don't you just get on with your future?"

"You mean exist on love alone? Forget trust? Who needs to worry that her husband might decide he's had enough again in another few months?"

"So you don't trust him. You love him. A lot. You're afraid to tell him no, because you know he's not going to give up. And now he's on his feet, maybe shaky, but I figure he's going to camp on our porch until you agree to work this out."

"I am afraid. Afraid I'll say yes and we'll get back together and this thing will always be there."

"No, kid," Stacey said softly. One finger tapped gently at Casey's temple. "Here. Until you talk with Zach, hear his story, it'll stay there. Growing by the day, eating away at your happiness, feeding your insecurities—destroying you and him. What will your private duty stint hurt?"

"I know this whole plot is silly. I keep thinking everything will solve itself if we just leave it alone and that's even sillier. Tonight, Stacey. I'll decide tonight."

Stacey watched Casey leave the room before picking up the phone.

"What's she doing?" Zach asked.

"Trying to talk me into pretending to be her and telling you no."

"Scared?" he guessed.

"Running fast and hard, but tonight's the night. She's making her decision."

"For or against?" He made no attempt to hide his hopefulness.

"I can't say. I'm leaning toward 'for,' but maybe that's my romantic streak breaking through."

"Romantic streak? You?"

Stacey smiled at his hoot of laughter. "Funny, isn't it?"

"I hope not."

"A little romance and a lot of love never hurt anything. Of course if I were you, I'd start polishing up the truth. No fables. No blarney. Just the plain old truth. Straight from the hip. She's a sucker for honesty. Why am I telling you this? I just might suggest she make you wear a hair shirt for a while."

"For Casey I would."

"I don't think she would go that far."

❧

Casey wandered around her bedroom, touching the various articles Zach had sent her since his return. Everything Stacey said had merit. Couples fought every day. Okay, so maybe one didn't claim he was making a decision that was best for them both and walk out. But in Zach's mind, whatever the reason, Casey knew it had been something he was truly incapable of handling.

What had happened since then? Had the problem righted itself? Or was she going to face another dilemma when he finally told her the whole story?

She sank onto a chair and let her mind drift back to happier times.

❧

"How long, Stacey?"

"Patience, Zach," she warned. Casey had been upstairs for a couple of hours. "It took you a few days to come to a decision. It may be the same for Casey."

"I hope not. I don't think I can bear much more of this waiting. It's driving me up the wall."

"Got to go," she said hurriedly when Casey called her name. "I think the jury's in. Good luck."

"You'll let me know?"

"With any luck, she will."

"That would be a miracle."

"Maybe not so much of one as you think. In here," Stacey called as she replaced the receiver.

"Who was on the phone?"

"A friend. Well?"

"You're right. As usual," Casey added with a grimace. "Either way I end up kicking myself."

"Casey?"

"It's true. If I say no and lose Zach and then one day find out I was wrong, I kick myself. If I go back and I'm happy for a while and it ends, I kick myself. I hurt either way, but maybe if it happens again I'll have something more of Zach than honeymoon memories. I think maybe I should find out what this has really been about before I throw in the towel. If there is still an *us* after that, maybe our marriage will grow. Who knows? Maybe a little more love and nurturing on my part and hopefully not all fertilizer on his."

"Give him a hard time, sis. Make him do everything you always wanted. He's romanced you his way. Make him romance you in yours."

"I'd be a fool not to want the romance, but I need more. I want our marriage to have substance. I want him to talk to me. And I want a baby."

"Don't just listen to him. Make him listen to you too."

Casey reached for her purse. "I plan to. Zach says he wants me back. I wonder if he'll feel the same after I tell him what I want."

❧

"Casey, what are you doing here at this time of night?"

She crossed the room and stopped beside the bed, pulling the string that controlled the light over the bed. The fluorescent bulb flickered to life, bringing a surge of artificial light into the room. She had to see him. There wasn't going to be any hiding in the shadows. "If I agree to be your nurse, what do you think is going to happen?"

"Whatever you want."

"That pat answer won't work."

"Okay, I hope we can make our marriage real again. I've missed having you in my arms."

"Is it the sex?"

"No," Zach cried, grabbing her hand and drawing it to his chest. "It's feeling like I'll die if you aren't part of my life again."

"So it's an opportunity to redeem yourself?"

"No. I love you. I want a life with you. Running away only proved how necessary it is."

"It took you two weeks to make that decision?"

"It took me one day to realize I couldn't face life without you. I spent the next week telling myself I had to be fair to you. I was coming home to tell you the truth when I had the accident. You weren't called because I told them we were separated. I couldn't come back to you as a physical cripple. There's a hope you won't have to contend with that now. Just the mental cripple I've become."

"You realize it won't happen overnight." At his nod, she asked, "Why the lake? Why not our house here in Wilmington?"

"I want to sell the house. Buy one of those drafty old places you love so much and help with the restoration. It's time I had a hobby."

"And just when do we do this?"

"Whenever you want. You call the shots. You can take a leave of absence or we can work on it on our days off."

"You aren't playing fair."

"I'm not playing, Casey," Zach stressed. "We lived in my house even though I knew you wanted a different place."

"I didn't see it that way. There were practical considerations to living in the house you owned. We had all the time in the world for the changes. But there's something I want more, Zach."

Hopeful eagerness covered his handsome face.

"A child," Casey stated. "I want to start a family."

His head dropped back on the pillows as he stared at her through suddenly glassy eyes.

Pain clutched its fingers about her body and squeezed tightly. *He doesn't want children. That was why he left.*

"Can we talk about this after you hear what I have to tell you?" he asked, the words tight with his anguish.

"We can talk, but I'm being honest, Zach. One way or the other, I plan to have a child of my own. If you don't want to be the father, tell me now. Don't hurt me again."

"There's nothing in the world I'd like more," he answered truthfully. "Just hold me, Casey. I've felt so alone."

four

Solitude.

It's like coming home after a long spell of homesickness, Zach thought as he watched Casey lift a box of groceries from the SUV's tailgate. Being here, having her with him, almost seemed a fantasy. It was a good place to start their rebuilding.

The house was actually more of a cabin—a family room-kitchen combination with one bedroom and bath downstairs, and a loft bedroom and bath upstairs. Walls of glass looked out over an old-fashioned wraparound porch facing the lake, providing the inhabitants with an incredible view.

The man-made lake sat in the midst of one hundred acres of prime real estate belonging to the Taylor family. Their retreat lacked nothing. The lake was a water lover's paradise with its pier, boathouse, huge slide, long ropes hanging from the tall pines, and fish. The grounds boasted a tennis court, bicycling/walking track, even a miniature golf course.

The May day was beautiful with above normal temperatures in the high eighties, and rays of the big bright sun glittering on the ruffled surface of the water. A slight breeze shifted the leaves on the trees while birds sang lustily from their branches.

"I should be carrying those," Zach protested from a rocker on the porch.

Casey shifted her hold on the box and flashed him a no-nonsense look. "The only things you're going to lift are your crutches. Don't think for one moment you're home free because David agreed I could handle your therapy. One wrong move could have you back in traction."

As his gaze drifted over her, Zach thanked God for a second chance. He'd always considered her to be his good luck pixie. So tiny and determined, usually bemoaning her little girl cuteness, today Casey was dressed in a short romper suit and looked every bit of the woman she was. Everything about her made him want to forget his injuries.

But Zach knew his body and his wife weren't ready yet. In time, they would resume the intimacy of their marriage. Just as in time he'd explain why he wouldn't father a child. Casey would understand. She'd agree that as long as they had each other, things would be perfect.

The screen door closed with a little bang as she came out of the house. "Just two more boxes and my suitcases. I'll fix lunch and then unpack this afternoon. Luckily, the place has been cleaned."

"I told Mom we were coming. She probably had the caretaker put a little extra polish on everything."

"I love this place. You're lucky to be able to come here whenever you want."

"The best time was our honeymoon."

"I'll get the rest of our things."

"Casey, don't," he called as she all but darted off the porch. "If you don't want me to say those things, tell me. Don't run away."

She turned to face him. "I'm not running. It was special for me too. One of the many wonderful times we shared. I guess that's why I can't. . . I'd better get those boxes. Daylight's burning."

Zach slammed his hand against the rocker arm. He'd made her cry. *Why did I open my big mouth?* "Casey, I'm sorry," he said when she came up the steps again. "I never meant to upset you."

"One step at a time," she said. "First we get you back on your feet. We have time for the rest. How about tuna for lunch? There are a couple of boiled eggs in the cooler."

"Pita pockets?" he asked hopefully.

A faint smile curved Casey's mouth. "What else? There's also lettuce and tomato."

"And shall we dine alfresco?"

"But of course. That's one of the best things. Bright sun, gentle breezes, and birds singing. I feel almost serene just thinking about it."

She returned several minutes later carrying a tray.

"Hold this." Casey went back inside to drag a small table onto the porch.

A slight smile touched Zach's lips as she arranged the food so that he could reach it easily. *Always the nurse.*

Casey settled into the companion rocker and reached for her sandwich. "How are your parents?"

We sound like strangers. Zach grimaced at the thought that his careless action had taken them so far from the loving couple they had been. He sipped the iced tea. "Mom said everything's great. Dad's negotiating a deal to buy another hotel, and if all goes well, Taylor Enterprises will soon have number five."

"Five. Seems like only yesterday they were buying the first."

Zach nodded. "Dad said they spend so much time in hotels, they might as well be the ones making the profit."

There was silence as both concentrated on their food. Finished, Casey drew her feet up into the chair, resting her chin on her knees. "Mom and Dad stay at their hotels sometimes. They really like the personal touch your parents added. Have you ever wanted to travel like they do?"

His gaze lingered on her. "Is that what you'd like to do? We could plan a long trip. Just the two of us."

"Not now. What I meant was did you ever want to be in business with them?"

"Not really. I'm too attached to my medicine. Once I got over the shock of their leaving, I realized theirs was not the life for me. I prefer having a base. Besides, my practice requires staying in place. Then I met you and had another reason to stay in Wilmington. Still, I admit I was surprised when they sold the house."

"But not Solitude."

Zach noted the way Casey's eyes did a quick circle of the area before coming back to him. "They love it as much as you do. I think they'll retire here one day."

She reached for her tea glass. "Mom and Dad were like your parents. For as long as Stacey and I needed them, they were there. Then they turned the shop over to a manager, put the house into our hands, and headed for everywhere. I hope Stacey's taking care of things. Sometimes I doubt she cares how valuable the antiques are."

"Your precious antiques." The words slipped out as he recalled the exhaustive searches for every piece. Granted they were lovely, heirloom quality. His wife's passion. She could read and talk about them for hours. He'd seen her excitement grow in her study of a quality piece until she almost forgot his existence. Oh, she'd attempted to include him, but Zach had never shared her passion for antiques. Just his own for her.

"Not mine. Mom and Dad's."

"You never took yours from the house?"

"No. Just my clothes. Stacey was in the guest house and there was room for me. It was convenient to the hospital, well-decorated. We didn't need our. . .my furniture."

Zach caught the correction. He'd considered himself to be pretty conscientious when he'd had his attorney draw up papers giving her all the furniture in the house. It had meant more to her and he had believed that it would somehow soften the blow.

"Did you ever. . .?" he broke off, unsure how to phrase the question. "Did you think I'd come back?" he blurted finally.

"At first I hoped you might. I had this crazy idea it was all a bad dream. That you'd come home and things would return to normal. After a couple of days, I believed it was over."

"I'm sorry."

Her gaze rested on him, the velvet brown eyes wide with hurt. "I never wanted your apologies," she choked out. "I wanted your love. I wanted you." She sprang from the chair. "I'm going for a walk. We'll start your therapy when I get back."

Zach longed to call her back, but knew he couldn't. He'd touched a nerve with that stupid question and right now she needed privacy. Time to recoup. Time to heal. Why hadn't he told her everything?

How would Casey react to learning he planned to start a research center? Would she understand he had to make a difference? That had been the primary reason behind his decision to specialize in pediatric medicine. Healthy children became healthy adults. He wanted to research pediatric diabetes—to explore the ramification that had been thrust into his conscious realization. The reason why he would never father a child.

He had been older when he discovered he had the disease, but he understood how it affected its victims, young and old. He knew how hated the daily injections became, had experienced the mood swings, tolerated the diet restrictions. So often he'd been forced to eat healthy foods when all he wanted was an ice cream sundae. At least he'd known a normal childhood. Not like some children he'd treated who were burdened for the rest of their young lives, their bodies refusing to provide the needed insulin. It was so unfair. If only he could make a difference. For the children and for Casey.

❧

Casey wandered along the bike path that ran through the woods around the lake. Maybe she should have stayed and talked with Zach, but she was also determined that their time together wasn't going to be spent rehashing the past.

She couldn't tell him how angry his actions had made her. She'd been so enraged by the document he'd sent giving her the furniture that she'd shredded the pages. Stacey had gathered the sheets and taped them together, forcing her to see sense as she put them out of sight.

He promised to explain. She promised to listen. Then together they would make a decision as to whether they had a future together.

Sure, he could excite her as no man ever had. Her body reacted normally to his loving looks even though her brain said no go.

They had hours of talking to do. Maybe for the first time during their marriage she might understand her husband. He certainly owed her an explanation for his inexplicable behavior.

Casey stopped walking. None of this was helping. It was time for his therapy. Then she had to unpack and make the beds. Zach would use the downstairs bedroom. She'd take the loft.

Where has he gone? she wondered as she rounded the corner and found the porch empty. *Surely not in search of me.* Her steps quickened as she took the steps two at a time, her heart thudding as she threw open the door, a fine edge of fear threading her voice. "Zach? Where are you?"

"Here, Casey. In the family room."

She walked through the archway from the entry hall, around the sofa to find him lying on the floor, his crutches propped against the armchair. "What are you doing?"

"I started the exercises."

"You should have waited."

"I know the routine. I've done it enough."

"Never unsupervised."

"I didn't bring you here to work. So far, you've unloaded the car and fixed lunch. You still have to unpack. This is all I can handle. At least let me do that much."

"Work," Casey pshawed, kneeling by his side. "I'm enjoying myself. Did you do the leg lifts?"

"Do I have to?"

"Now you see why it's supervised. You only want to do the easy stuff. Luckily, you'll be able to use the stairs for your knee exercises."

"Lucky for whom?"

Casey stifled a giggle.

Zach was sweating profusely when he completed the last round of exercises. "Keep that up and you'll soon be walking better than ever," Casey said as she helped him up and placed a towel about his neck.

"We can hope."

"We can believe." Her voice was firm, final, as her hand rested on his arm. "Now, no more nice guy. You're right about needing to do your share. Dinner's your baby. The wok's on the counter. The ingredients for stir-fry are in the refrigerator. There's also a handy bar stool. Just don't burn yourself."

Casey was reminded of the klutz Zach became in the kitchen. He used every pot and always managed to burn himself. Sometimes she thought it was just so she'd kiss it better. She hardened her heart to the hopeful look in the blue eyes.

"I'll make the beds. After dinner, you can unpack your things."

Later, she lay in bed watching the night through the skylight. A full moon. There had been a full moon on their wedding night.

Funny how things had changed since then. That night she had felt they were as close as a man and woman could get. But they had grown even closer, or so she'd thought. Casey had thought being separated was tough, but knowing he was downstairs in another bed and they were still apart was even harder.

Well, there was always tomorrow. One day at a time, and today hadn't been as tough as she'd thought it would be.

five

The sun had climbed high in the sky when Casey woke the next morning. She yawned and stretched against the comfortable mattress, unable to summon the energy needed to get out of bed.

Her body just wasn't geared to early days, and ordinarily she would attribute her lassitude to working the graveyard shift. Last night's sleeplessness had to do with the thoughts that had claimed her consciousness.

Zach seemed so different, so determined to make amends. Too determined. He'd hurt her terribly with his desertion. She'd never been so alone, felt so desolate as she had night after night during their separation.

It had been a little better when she'd moved into the guest house, away from her memories. At least there had been someone to talk to, someone who understood she needed to get on with her life. Stacey had refused to let her dwell in the past.

If only they could continue from that last morning. She wouldn't have minded not having to agonize through the memories of being apart. In fact, Casey preferred to start from the moment Zach, still flushed from their lovemaking, had kissed her good-bye and told her he loved her.

But they weren't in a time warp and it wasn't going to happen. Casey stretched and yawned again, fighting the temptation to linger. She had to wake up. Zach was downstairs, and he'd probably been awake since six, waiting as patiently as he knew how. And from experience she knew he had no surplus of that capacity.

A quick shower would take care of the lingering sandman. Then maybe she could convince Zach to take her out on the lake. He'd always loved the boat. They had spent hours drifting along, talking, loving. Casey shook her head as the memories poured in. *Forget the loving. For now we need to talk.*

Just in case, Casey put on a one-piece swimsuit and a pair of shorts. She flipped a comb through her damp hair and ran downstairs.

"Morning," she called, coming to a halt at the sight of Zach stretched out on the couch. He wore jeans, his short-sleeved print shirt unbuttoned and his feet bare. The crutches lay on the floor by the chair. "Did you have a good night?"

"The usual," he allowed, somewhat despondently. "You?"

Casey yawned, a smile lighting the eyes over her hand as she covered her open mouth. "I'm used to going to bed during the day. It took me a while to get to sleep. Did you eat?"

"I wasn't hungry."

Something was wrong here. The Zach she knew ate on a regular schedule, burning off calories with his hectic lifestyle. "Are you in pain?"

"My leg," he said after a momentary hesitation.

"Think a massage would help? Pull your pants leg up. I'll get the lotion."

She should have known yesterday would be a bit much. First the trip and then the therapy. Maybe they should wait a day or so before he started up again. No need in setting his recuperation back.

Casey poured a pool of lotion into her hand to warm as she stepped from the bedroom and almost dropped the bottle at the sight of Zach in only his underwear. Her lids dropped and she shook her head to clear the vision before studying him with a more clinical eye. His ribs were more prominent.

"Zach," she warned.

"Those jeans had straight legs. I can't even pull my socks up when I wear them."

"Didn't you bring your running shorts?"

"I couldn't find them."

No sense in making a big deal of this. She'd seen him in the white briefs so often she could visualize his athletic physique, the compact, well-muscled body with her eyes closed. He had a great body, his few hours of exercise each week paying off in major dividends.

"I'll find them later. It'll be too hot to wear jeans all day."

Casey dropped to her knees by the sofa and began to massage his injured leg. She felt the rough textures of hair and muscled male skin as she worked her hands along the length of his leg, the longing stirring deep within her. She hesitated at the ridge of tissue where they had sewn his leg up. "They did a good job, but you'll still have a scar."

Zach could have purred with contentment as Casey worked her wonders. The pain had awakened him early that morning and he had fought it, refusing to take the medication. He was so tired of being half alive. And now that he was with Casey again, he needed to focus all his faculties on her.

Still, it was almost worth the pain to have her hands on him again. The tiny, well-shaped fingers glided ever so softly over his leg, comforting, warming, and pleasing.

Her use of her hands had always been expressive. They moved when she talked and communicated in other ways. Angel-of-mercy hands, he had called them, recalling their ability to restore pleasure to his world.

He had been so glad to find she was a toucher. Bad days never seemed quite so bad when Casey smiled at him and touched his cheek or massaged the tenseness from his neck. Good days were even more so when she—

"Zach?" She surprised him, and he leaped like a startled

gazelle before his gaze focused fuzzily.

"Is the cramp gone?"

Lost in her beautiful soul-searching gaze, he stared. How could he have hurt her as he had? It made no sense now. This was the woman he loved. The woman he wanted to spend his life with. A threatening knot blocked his throat as his eyes moistened. Would he lose her with the truth?

"Zach? Are you okay? You're acting weird."

He sighed as her hands worked out the recurring spasm. "Lack of sleep," he murmured as he captured her tiny hand and brought it to his lips. "I love these fingers."

"Oh."

Brilliant, he mocked silently when she pulled her hand back to rest in her lap.

"I was going to suggest we take the boat out, but you'd better rest. You probably should have skipped your therapy yesterday. Because of the trip and all."

Zach struggled up, his grimace fraught with misery as he pushed his legs off the sofa. "No. Therapy yesterday, today, tomorrow, every waking moment, if that's what it takes to get me back on my feet."

"Or off them forever," Casey argued, holding him in place with her hands on his shoulders. "You will not overdo, Zachary Taylor. We will approach your therapy sensibly, or I'll tell your doctor you're an uncooperative patient."

"You would," he said with a sheepish grin. "Casey, you know what I mean. I knew about the cramps. David warned me."

She settled back, disappointed. "Why didn't you tell me?"

"You just did all you could to alleviate the pain. It's passed now. Let's talk about the boat."

"Let's talk about a muscle relaxer for you and a couple of chairs on the pier," Casey injected stubbornly. "A lazy, peaceful day with no overexertion for either of us. Maybe the boat after you've recuperated a bit more."

"I can handle it, Casey."

"Fine." She threw her hands into the air and turned away. "Go. Have a wonderful time. Just don't expect any help from me."

"Casey?" The plaintive cry followed her into the kitchen. She ignored him and began preparing her breakfast. "Yuck," Zach groaned as she dumped ingredients for a protein shake into the blender. She added banana slices and bran and depressed the button.

"It wouldn't hurt you to drink this," Casey said as she poured the concoction into a glass and added a straw.

Lately it seemed she had cultivated a certain smile, he thought as she looked at him. Not the warm, love-filled ones of their marriage, but not the forced ones he expected.

"Okay."

The word stopped her dead in her tracks. Zach had never sampled the shakes before, claiming he'd rather eat dirt.

She passed him the glass and poured the remainder into another for herself. As she sipped, Casey watched him watch her, slightly unnerved by the love that burned so strong in his eyes.

If she lived to be one hundred, she'd never forget the way he could make her melt with that look. But she had to be strong. Falling into his arms now wouldn't solve a thing. Maybe this closeness was bad for them both.

Zach set his glass on the countertop and moved ever so slightly, putting himself within easy reach.

"Zach, no."

"I've been a good boy. Just one little kiss."

What could it hurt? Just one to see if the old magnetism had disappeared when he'd broken her heart.

Have you gone mad? a little voice deep inside her brain demanded as Casey shortened the distance.

Little kisses had unbelievable potency, Casey discerned as their lips met and clung. The kiss sang through her veins. It was no different from the first time, every bit as special. Their first evening together had made Casey pretty certain he was the man for her, but their first kiss had confirmed it.

Her arms slid about his neck, the kiss continuing as he wrapped her in his arms. Both were breathless as they pulled apart and stared at each other, trying to gauge an understanding of where they stood.

"Where did you go?" The question was whispered as she moved slightly away.

A strange, faintly eager look flashed into his eyes. "Here." Perhaps it was simply his uneasiness, or maybe that the eyes that met his were misty and wistful. "Because I was confused. Scared." Zach awkwardly cleared his throat. "I can't give you children." At her stunned look, he exclaimed, "That's why I left. I was going to keep it a secret."

The import of his words curled like tentacles into her brain, squeezing so tightly Casey felt overwhelmed by hopelessness. "Are you positive?" At his nod, she argued, "There are doctors. Specialists. Tests."

"I am a doctor, Casey."

"You? You made a self-diagnosis? You're a pediatrician. How could you possibly be certain?"

"Casey, it's not a medical problem." At her confused look, Zach said, "I lost a patient."

What was he saying? Why would losing a patient mean they couldn't have children? "I'm sorry, but it happens."

"I tried to tell myself that. I struggled to believe I'd done everything in my power to save him, but this time it didn't make a difference. He was eleven, Casey. Deprived of life when he had so much living to do, so much to see."

"What do you want to hear, Zach?" she asked, drawing

from the reserve deep inside her as she fought to understand what he was trying to tell her. "You knew from the moment you decided to become a doctor that you couldn't save everyone. You've had a very high success rate. What made this one so difficult?"

"It all had to do with you."

She took a quick breath of utter astonishment. What had she done? "Me?" she repeated in a small, frightened voice.

"No, not you." His face clouded with uneasiness. "What you wanted. That morning you'd barely kissed me hello before asking when we could start a family."

"You didn't object then. Why does the thought terrify you so now?" she asked, half in anticipation, half in dread.

"That child was an undiagnosed diabetic, Casey. He went into a coma and died." Both knew he'd suffered since his diagnosis twelve years ago. He'd lived through the highs and lows, and cursed the chronic disease for which there was no cure. Only control. "There's nothing in the world I want more than to have a baby with you, but all I can think of is afflicting our child with this terrible disease."

"You could have talked to me. And asked God for guidance instead of going it all alone."

The tortured disbelief in his eyes broke her heart. "Believe me, I prayed. I knew that. I also knew how badly you wanted a child, but I honestly don't see how we. . .how I can father a child."

"You're a doctor, Zach. You know the likelihood of a child inheriting your diabetes. With control, we're not talking life-threatening."

The guarded expression didn't disguise the burst of anger in the depths of his blue gaze. "It's unfair to bring a child into the world to have to contend with illness. You're twenty-eight, Casey. Ready to have a child. You wouldn't stop to think about the consequences."

Casey listened with rising dismay. "Okay, so maybe I can be relentless when it comes to something I want, but no more so than the next person. In all fairness to me, have I ever refused to listen to what you had to say?"

"No, but there was nothing you'd ever wanted so badly. I was afraid you wouldn't agree the diabetes was reason enough to wait."

"Why should I? You've been so determined to shield me from your illness." Casey sucked in a deep breath, unable to dislodge the heaviness centered in her chest as she plunged on. "I found out about the insulin reaction from Donald. I knew something was wrong, but it never occurred to you to tell me, did it?"

"Casey, I—"

"What did you think I'd do? Demand you quit working so hard? Of course, I couldn't do that since we didn't discuss your work either. That's the really hard part. Wanting you to share your feelings and knowing you won't. You acted as if we left our careers at the hospital and turned into different people at home. I think this proves we didn't. The joys and sorrows came with us. The joys added to our lives but the sorrows hung over our heads, making us miserable. All because we never talked."

"I'm not a talker, Casey. You know that. I love you. I didn't want to burden you with my problems."

"Think again, Zach. You burdened us both by refusing to talk it out. It wasn't fair."

"I never knew."

She managed to shrug and say, offhandedly, "There's no sense in rehashing it now."

"There's every sense. I came back because I don't want to lose you, Casey."

Fear, stark and vivid, glittered in her eyes. "And you were almost killed before you could. All because you lied and ran away. You broke my heart, Zachary Taylor." A hot tear trickled down her face and Casey spun about and ran from the room, determined to escape. She would never understand this man she'd married.

Zach stared after her. He'd been protecting her. He'd thought that by keeping his burdens to himself he would make it easier on them both. But he'd been wrong. If he'd stayed and faced up to her with his true feelings about fathering a child, he wouldn't be suffering such great mental and physical pain.

The hours stretched infinitely as Zach waited for Casey's return. At least he knew she was upstairs in her bedroom. There hadn't been any movement in the loft, so he didn't think she was packing. And he prayed she wasn't crying. He couldn't bear making her cry.

Zach was tempted to navigate the stairs but recognized he'd end up in a heap at the bottom. Maybe one or two steps, but never the two short flights. He'd give her a little longer and then he would sit on the bottom step and call out until she had no other choice but to respond.

&a.

Casey laid the photo album on the bed. It had been silly of her to bring it, but she had this hope that the memories might make them happy again. A totally unrealistic thought maybe, but desperate people took desperate measures.

Why had she run off in tears? Hadn't he just done what she'd wanted him to do? Zach had told her why he left and where he had gone. For the first time, they had actually talked about a problem, and this time, *she* had run away.

It was senseless to hide herself away up here. Knowing Zach, she'd drive him to doing something stupid. Like trying to climb the stairs.

Casey slipped on flip-flops before making a detour by the bathroom to pick up a couple of towels. She went downstairs, catching his gaze on her as she walked into his bedroom and began sorting through the clothes he hadn't bothered to unpack.

She refolded a couple of pieces and placed them in the drawer. They would be here for at least four weeks and he couldn't live out of a suitcase forever. She looked up as he came to stand in the doorway. "There's a pair of shorts on the bed. Swim trunks in the top drawer."

"Casey?"

"Not now, Zach."

Casey frowned at the tumbled pile of clothing in the suitcase and swiped the sudden surge of tears from her eyes. She loved Zach, but staying with him meant she'd never become a mother. Her legs weakened and she sank to the bed, groaning as she muffled the sobs that came from her throat in rapid succession. It was so unfair.

He recognized the strain in her voice and knew now was not the time to discuss the matter further. Maybe it didn't make sense. But he'd told her the plain old truth, exactly as Stacey had instructed.

Zach steadied himself on the crutches, the sight of her shoulders shaking as she hid her face in his shirt stopping him from moving forward. He'd done this to her. Loving him had taken away another of her dreams. He'd already destroyed their chances at happy ever after. Why not let her go? Give her the chance to find happiness again?

He moved as quickly as possible, maneuvering himself to the bed and rolling across the distance to capture her in his arms. "Casey honey, I'm so sorry."

Her face came to rest against his neck, the tears liquid warmth as they trailed over his bare skin.

"Sweetie, please don't cry. We can find an answer together. Just don't cry. I love you, Casey," Zach whispered, his fingers tenderly erasing the signs of her tears. "I'll let you go so you can make a good life for yourself. One with children."

"I don't want another man's children, Zachary Taylor," she cried out, pounding her clenched fist against his chest. "I want yours, and I won't give up hope until I've consulted every doctor in the country if I have to. If what you believe is true, I'll accept that there's no chance. But if there's a hope in this world that I can mother your child, we'll have a baby or my name is not Casey Bordeaux-Taylor."

❧

Why doesn't she settle down? Zach asked himself as he listened to Casey perform her nightly routine.

The routine. How well he remembered her preparations for bed. First the exercises, exactly thirty minutes, and then the bath, usually scented with her one extravagance, a perfumed bath oil that he always thought of as Casey's scent.

Afterward she creamed her body before slipping into her nightwear, often things he had chosen. When she told him she loved the fact that he didn't consider himself too macho to buy them, he had brought home a new outfit almost every week. Zach suddenly felt like a voyeur as he pictured her in the outfits, ones she had worn to please. Probably now she wore an old cotton T-shirt to bed every night.

Casey had been determined to be a good wife, from the moment she descended the stairs to become his bride until the moment she'd begged him to explain before he walked out.

Pity he didn't know how to be a good husband. Too secretive and then he'd hurt her—in the name of love. Wasn't he right to want to protect her?

He admired his wife in so many ways. She was strong and

courageous and beautiful. Casey was the type of person who cared about people, who gave of herself selflessly and whole-heartedly.

She didn't stint in the loving department. She gave and gave, and he was afraid of how worrying about her child would affect her. Could she bear fighting a disease that lasted a life-time and required constant attention? She would suffer the full spectrum of intense emotions with her child.

Was he being selfish? Zach only knew he didn't want any-thing killing their love and their marriage day by day. He loved her too much for that.

There were more footsteps and then a knock at his door before her head popped around the door. "Did you take the medicine, Zach?"

"I don't want to."

She smiled at his grumpy words. "Take it anyway. The muscle relaxers will keep you from being in pain."

"They make me too drowsy."

Casey came further into the room and Zach swallowed hard at the flash of satin tap pants coupled with a matching camisole underneath the unbelted toweling robe.

"Take them and I'll stay and talk."

He threw back the sheet and started to sit up. "I'll have to get water."

Casey waved him back. "I'll get it. Where are the pills?"

"In the drawer." *She is going to stay and I won't be able to keep my eyes open,* Zach thought as he tugged the drawer pull. He shook the required dosage into his hand.

"Here you go," Casey said as she passed him the glass. Automatically she fluffed the pillows before gesturing him back. "I'll sit here so I won't have to talk so loud."

As she curled up on the edge of the bed, Zach allowed his gaze to drift over her face. "Aren't you tired?"

"Not really. It'll take a while for my system to adjust from sleeping during the day." She laughed softly and said, "Probably about the time I have to go back to work."

"Probably," he murmured, breathing deeply as the perfume wafted with her movement.

"I never thought I'd like the night shift as much as I do. I manage to get so much more done. I don't need eight hours of sleep, so I can go over to the shop to check incoming stock and talk with browsers."

Zach hated the growing drowsiness. "You always were a big hit with the customers. Except for that one couple who used to drive you up the wall." A tiny smile formed on his lips. "Remember? You'd drag every piece into the light for them and give them all the history."

Casey's laughter was infectious, always inviting the listener to join in. "We've got a contest going in the shop. I say they'll never buy. Ben's working overtime in his quest to sell them something. He gets a day off if he does."

"Hope your luck holds."

"It has for several weeks now." She glanced out the window. "The weatherman predicted sun tomorrow. We might be able to swim. Wonder if I can get a floating lounge chair into the lake?"

"Not alone," Zach muttered, frustrated when a huge yawn interrupted his words. "I'll call Jake to take it out for you."

"I can call him. Go to sleep," she whispered. Her fingers closed over his arm, squeezing gently as her thumb stroked back and forth. "I've talked enough."

"You always loved to talk."

"It always amazed me that such a quiet person could be attracted to a blabbermouth."

"Can you imagine me with another non-talker? It would be worse than a silent film festival."

"Personally, I love the strong, silent type. Now, I'd better get out of here and let you sleep."

"Just a few more minutes," he pleaded, capturing her hand when she started to rise. "I like having you near."

And she liked being near. Suddenly her lonely bed lacked appeal. They had made it through another day, and, hopefully, their future would extend to many more. Today's talking had given them an idea of where they were headed. Zach twisted on the bed, making himself more comfortable. Casey slid downward and then shifted to give him space. She really should go. He needed to rest. It had been a hard day for a recuperative patient.

Just another minute. Zach retained his hold, threading their fingers together before he slept. It was a comforting sensation. The closeness she had dreamed of for far too many nights was hers. The quiet added to Casey's peace, and she lay absorbing the sound of his relaxed breathing.

That had been another of the things she had missed while they were apart. She'd grown so accustomed to his sleeping habits. So many nights she'd awakened alone, certain she could feel him in bed next to her.

Carefully, she slid an arm over his chest, as close to a hug as she could manage. A satisfied smile curved her lips. He was here and she didn't have to let him go. Not yet.

So Casey didn't, and the night claimed yet another willing victim as she slept with her love in her arms.

six

"Knock it off down there," Casey yelled, clutching the pillow about her ears and groping for her watch. In the bright morning light of summer, she determined it was six A.M. Okay, so clocks were taboo at Solitude. Everyone kept their own schedule, and they were on a sort of vacation. But why couldn't Zach settle down for a few more hours?

"Casey? Can you hear me?"

She sighed at the restless call of her mate. "They can hear you in Wilmington."

"I'm going to take a little walk around the place. Check out the wildlife."

"Oh, no, you're not." Casey scrambled from the bed and raced to the stair landing to find Zach propped against the carved newel post at the bottom. "The only wildlife you'll see today is from the porch. In the rocker, the hammock, anywhere you like, so long as it's sitting or lying down. You will not go stumbling about this terrain and undo all the good we've accomplished."

"But Casey—"

"But nothing. If you're in such great need of exercise, start your therapy. And don't leave out the—"

"I know the routine," Zach interrupted. "It's boring—the same thing day in, day out."

Casey fought back a smile. He'd be horrified to know he sounded exactly like one of his pediatric patients.

"Adults are supposed to have longer attention spans, Zachary. If you're bored, be creative. Count differently. Play

72

word games. There are cassettes in the library if you'd prefer exercising to music."

"How about a kiss every time I finish the set?"

As creative ideas go, that's not too bad, Casey admitted, her eyelashes fluttering against her cheeks. "Better yet, why don't you find a book and read for an hour or so?"

He seemed disappointed by her reluctance to keep him company. "I've read everything, including several books in my Bible."

"When?" Casey asked, incredulous at the thought of him going through the dozen or so books he'd brought along.

"Over the last two weeks. During all those hours I've spent on the porch, in the rocker, in the hammock, on the couch, in bed. Please, Casey. Just a little walk."

"I'll have to pick up more reading material," she said. "Wait, I have a mystery you haven't read."

He wailed her name as she darted off. Casey lifted the book from her nightstand and wavered. She'd never known Zach to read so much. Suddenly, Casey understood Zach's restlessness. No wonder he was stir-crazy. *Oh, why not? A short walk couldn't hurt, and if I supervise, even better.*

The book bounced on the mattress. In a matter of minutes, she dressed in a pair of white cotton pants and a rose off-the-shoulder blouse. Her sneakered feet pounded the stair treads as she ran down to join Zach.

"Don't just stand there," she told her surprised husband. "Get your walking shoes on. And don't forget the brace."

His smile was better than winning a gold medal, Casey decided. Satisfied, uninhibited, his one expression of unbridled happiness. It was no wonder she always worked so hard to make him smile.

Zach was back in record time. "How far, coach?"

"Depends on the terrain. To the pier, maybe two or three

times. Up the nature trail, a few hundred yards and back."

"Let's take the trail. I've seen the view from the pier too often."

The early morning silence enclosed them in its ambience, and neither did nor said anything to disturb the peaceful moments. After a while, as though an alarm went off, the woods awoke and came to life. Birds sang out, the trees soughed with the breeze, a twig snapped beneath a foot, and two squirrels chased each other across their path. The tiny creatures circled the trunk of a nearby pine and disappeared into the branches.

"I love these mornings," Zach whispered.

"It is nice," Casey agreed, stepping closer as she noted the uneven ground. Her hand hovered for a moment before she allowed herself to grasp his arm. "So I can keep up," she murmured when he looked at her. "You always forget my legs are shorter than yours."

He gripped the cane tightly. "I always felt like scooping you into my arms. Particularly when you wore heels."

Zach often found her efforts to appear taller hilarious. Casey smiled at the thought.

"What's that smile about?"

"Nothing," she denied hurriedly.

He chuckled, and she wanted him to kiss her. Casey missed his kisses, and that warm, loved feeling whenever he held her close. How would they ever work things out?

"Casey? Did you hear me?"

Surprised, she looked up at him. "I'm sorry. What?"

"How much farther?" Zach stared at her, seemingly baffled by her sudden distraction.

Casey glanced back, astonished to find the house out of sight. "Let's rest on this tree stump and then start back."

"I'm not tired," he protested when she patted the space

beside her. "Well, okay. There was something I wanted to tell you."

"Oh, Zach, do you have to—" she began, not wanting reality to intrude on this time.

"It's not what you think," he hurriedly explained. "I can wait. I just wanted to share something about my, well, hopefully *our,* future."

In that moment, Casey regretted her action. "Tell me," she invited softly, her hand sliding down his arm to take his hand in hers.

"I've been thinking about when we go back to Wilmington. I know my practice is waiting. Donald said whenever I was ready, my patients would be. But I need more. I need to feel I've accomplished something with my medicine. I want to apply for a research grant. I think we could handle it financially."

The words formulated in her head and for a few moments Casey struggled with the delight that coursed through her. *Zach has never discussed his career plans with me before.*

His practice was well established by the time they met. Casey recalled the first time she entered his office and found it seized with mothers wanting him for their kids. She knew how popular he was with the obstetric doctors from the numbers of times his name showed up on the newborn charts.

Everything she knew about him as a doctor came from a source other than her husband. Every approach about his work, his days, resulted in two words: "Nothing special." Never so much as one mention of a child he'd been taken with or agonized over.

Casey hadn't been able to maintain the same degree of objectivity. She talked about special patients, things that disturbed her, even cried in his arms when she'd grown too attached to a newborn that died.

"Any special area?"

"Pediatric diabetes. They have to live with the illness, and I'd like to take my shot at making it easier."

"What about other research in the field?"

"I've talked with a few people, written some letters." Zach's thumb brushed over her palm. "There's a strong probability I could get funding."

"Sounds as though you've made up your mind."

"No," he said quickly. Casey recognized the sudden apprehension in his eyes but was unable to respond before Zach rushed on. "This involves both of us. I want a second chance to make you happy. I'll do whatever it takes."

"Will you be able to keep all the promises, Zach? A new house, now a new career choice, but only if I approve. What if I told you I wanted the most expensive house in Wilmington and you to continue your practice?"

"I'd agree."

"Ha." The response slipped out before she could disguise her emotions. "I'm sorry, but I think you know me well enough to know I'll always support you in whatever makes you happy. That's what marriage is about. I don't care about *things*. For the record, I didn't mind living in your house. Just as you didn't mind that we furnished the place with antiques.

"Now you want to give me more possessions. You're even willing to give me the final say on your future and pretend you're happy so I'll be happy. I refuse to accept that. A second chance for our marriage won't be decided by whether you're financially able to provide my every want. Possessions have never been my priority. I need and want emotional support from the man you've kept hidden beneath the protective façade."

Zach squeezed her hand. "I'd like to be that man, but I wasn't raised to show my emotions. Dad always said it was a man's duty to protect his woman." He snorted derisively. "Then the first time I ever lost my objectivity, I acted like an idiot and skipped out. I disgust myself."

"You don't disgust me. You drive me to distraction with your secretive nature, but you never, ever disgust me. I only want to share your life. I knew you weren't the demonstrative type when we first met. My family life was entirely different. We discussed everything. Keeping that side of my nature under control has been a battle, but I did because I suspected it made you uncomfortable.

"You love your family," Casey continued. "It's not visible with hugs and kisses but in other ways, like being there for each other. When your Dad got sick during our honeymoon, I knew you had to go to him, but you kept apologizing and buying me things. I thought you'd eventually realize I didn't expect a gift every time a sharp word passed between us. You never did."

"Maybe I need to attend one of those get-in-touch-with-reality seminars?"

"No, my dear Zachary. Reality is the here and now. If we both hang in there, and seek God's guidance, our marriage stands a good chance. It ends the moment one of us decides it's too difficult."

A muscle quivered at his jaw. "I ran away because it was too difficult. Funny how being apart from you put things back into perspective."

"I'd like to think being with me could have accomplished the same thing." Casey stood and brushed off the seat of her pants. "I'm up for breakfast and watching you swim for an hour."

"Not another shake."

"Maybe half of one with bacon and eggs," she said. "Just for today, though."

Zach reached for her hand, adjusting his cane in the other hand. "Don't you worry I'll play on your sympathies and ask for bacon and eggs every morning?"

"I worry more that I'll run out of bran before our next run into Wilmington. Maybe I should call Stacey and have her go by the health food store before coming out."

"Maybe you should," Zach agreed complacently. "Actually, those shakes are beginning to grow on me. I think I've become leaner and meaner since I started drinking them."

Casey drew to a sudden halt. "How much?" she demanded, her hands going to his body to assess for herself. "You can't afford to lose any weight. Oh, you," she added as his grin spread. She tugged a whorl of the dark hair on his chest. "I ought to make you drink two for every meal."

His arms tightened about her. "Then my belly would get in the way whenever I hold you like this." His mouth swooped down to capture hers.

Casey didn't back away. Her arms slipped to his neck. "Let's don't ever leave each other again without a hug."

Zach leaned back to study her. "You think it'll help me show my emotions?"

"It'll help both of us to never regret the time we spend apart because we know how much we'll love each other when we're together again."

"I love you, Casey."

After breakfast, they relaxed in chairs on the porch. She glanced at Zach when the back and forth motion of the rocker drew to a standstill.

"I'm going to feed the ducks. Want to come?"

Casey's head barely moved against the glider's cushioned back. "I'm too comfortable."

She watched him move across the yard and down the pier. He was doing so much better. Every day seemed to bring an improvement, and the wrenching pain she'd felt at seeing him in agony had lessened as well. Still, there were times when she watched his slow gait and held back the tears of frustration at not being able to do more.

She loved Zach and wanted to do everything for him. Even now she sensed his growing agitation and wondered how long he would wait for her to make a decision.

A contented smile teased the corner of Casey's mouth. The decision was made. Zach would get his second chance, and a third or fourth if he needed. He was her mate for life, and Casey knew she'd work doubly hard to ensure their marriage lasted. His willingness to step out of her life if she couldn't live without a child told her exactly how much he cared.

"Lord, please help us find a solution to this other problem. And thank You for the miraculous healing You've brought to Zachary."

❧

Zach threw the handful of feed into the lake and watched idly as the ducks competed for it. What was she thinking right now? She hadn't said or done much since lunch, just lazed in the glider with her antique magazine, stopping now and then to discuss some tidbit she'd read.

He knew Casey was thinking and praying about their marriage, but he wanted an answer now. *Patience,* he cautioned as he looked back to reassure himself she was still there. God had worked on him for years to teach him that trait, and sometimes Zach wondered if he'd ever learn to wait for his Heavenly Father's will to be done.

Seek God's guidance. Casey's words of the morning came to him. Had he done that as he made plans for the future? He prayed but sometimes the urge to proceed was so strong he decided that was his answer from above.

He certainly needed God's guidance in how to proceed

here. Zach had never considered himself possessive, but over the last few days he'd grown to hate anything that stole her from him for any amount of time.

He turned back to the ducks. Why couldn't she forget what he had done? *Don't be a fool,* he thought with a flash of self-anger. *Why should she?* He couldn't. He'd never forgive himself for hurting Casey. He shouldn't have come back. If he'd stayed away, she could have had a chance at happiness with someone worthy of her.

"Greedy little beggars."

Zach jerked around as she spoke, her voice slightly louder than the ducks' raucous squawking.

"They'll eat us out of house and home."

"You could have chosen something practical like chickens. Eggs for breakfast and the makings of your favorite health food."

A smile creased his face. "Come on, Casey. You're scared to death of chickens. Remember the farm?"

"Well, they peck."

"I promised I'd protect you from the vicious little beasts if you protected me from Stacey."

"Since we never spent much time at poultry farms, it seems I got the more difficult task," she said, slipping her hand into the bag and scattering it over the water. Her laughter floated on the air as the ducks dived in.

"So much for my promises of protection. I let you down."

He turned away, and Casey surprised him by slipping her arms about his waist and resting her cheek against his back. Her hands moved over his chest. "That's the funny thing about life," she said. "We spend too much time analyzing and regretting. Just think how much better things would be if we concentrated on making the present better rather than trying to remake the past."

Zach fought his body's response to her nearness. He noted her deep, unsteady breath as she stepped back. "Isn't this a time to analyze and regret?"

He turned to face Casey, and her fingers touched the warmth of his outstretched hand.

"I love you. That hasn't changed. And we are moving toward making our marriage real again. I can explain, but now isn't the time. Stacey will be here soon."

He tilted his brow uncertainly. "After she goes?"

"By the time she leaves, you'll have your answer."

The bag fell unnoticed to the pier as Zach gathered her into his arms, one hand at the small of her back as his lips descended, demanding her full response.

❧

The screen door had barely shut when Casey rounded on her twin. "Why did you bring Zach's mother?"

"What was I supposed to do? She called yesterday morning. Asked if I'd heard from you two and invited herself along when I said I was coming up for the weekend."

Casey sighed as she led the way to the stairs. "I suppose she thinks I've had plenty of time to forgive Zach?"

"If I remember correctly, I think her words were 'Casey needs to teach him a lesson.' "

"Zach doesn't need to be taught anything. He just needs understanding. . ." Casey trailed off at Stacey's knowing grin and snapped, "You can wipe that smirk off your face."

"I'm sorry, Casey. I started to call her back and say the trip was off, but I couldn't. Mom and Dad need those papers by Monday afternoon and I don't have the faintest idea what they're talking about."

"Did you bring the chest?"

"In the car. The sooner you find them, the sooner we're out of your hair."

"Don't be silly," Casey chided. "There's no reason for you not to spend the weekend." She smiled at Stacey, coquettish as she whispered, "As for Zach and myself, it's inevitable."

"Not that look again." Stacey pushed a puzzled Casey toward the mirror. "That perpetual seventh heaven look when you're happy. What I'll never understand is why you always have to be coerced into everything. How long would you have waited if we hadn't come?"

Casey smiled. "Not long. He told me why. Now we have to figure out what we're going to do."

Stacey's forehead creased, concern overflowing into her words, "Is it bad?"

"Yes. The situation is going to require a lot of prayer." Casey knew she should probably tell Stacey the truth but she wasn't ready yet. She slipped an arm about her sister's waist and said, "Let's change and go for a swim. Have you redecorated the house yet?"

"The decorator comes tomorrow," Stacey joked, throwing one hand into the air. "He's renowned for his contemporary décor."

❧

Zach watched his wife with her twin as they walked out of the house laughing. The image fascinated him. Seeing them together always had. It was unbelievable that they could be so alike and so different, so attached. Maybe that was what he envied most. Casey's closeness to her sister was a spiritual thing. If only he understood his wife half as well.

At least he knew Casey well enough to recognize the burst of anger when his mother got out of Stacey's car. He knew the reason, and he'd sleep on the couch or in the car before he'd force Casey to share his bed. When she came to him, it would be her choice. He'd wait forever if necessary.

Casey sat on the arm of the rocker and slipped her arm

about his shoulders, her bright smile waking his body to full response. "Mind if I share your room tonight?"

His attempted nonchalance was a complete failure, his infectious grin setting the tone. "I'd love to have you."

"Why, Zachary Taylor," she drawled, her affected southern accent delighting him as she trailed her fingers over his arm, "the things you say."

The screen door squeaked and shut softly. "Casey, honey," Ellen Taylor called, "would you mind terribly if I took a nap before dinner? The jet lag and this heat have me so exhausted I can hardly keep my eyes open."

"Stop it," Casey whispered when Zach slipped a hand over the skin left exposed by her maillot. Pushing him away, she flashed her mother-in-law an understanding smile. "Not at all. Zach usually swims around this time and we're going to join him. Did you need help with your bag?"

Ellen shook her head. "The loft?"

Casey jumped to her feet. "Just let me move a few things."

Zach noted the dawning realization that lit his mother's eyes. "Oh, Casey, no. I'll take the couch."

"It's okay, Mom Taylor," Casey reassured, glancing at Zach as she pulled the screen door open. "Zach and I can share."

He listened to his mother's apologetic words, the resignation in her voice as she followed Casey inside. "I shouldn't have done this. I was always too protective when it came to my son. I wanted to know how he was doing. He wouldn't let me come to the hospital. Zachary never tells me anything. I thought you two had. . ."

Casey's response filled him with joy.

"We're going to make a go of our marriage and the first thing we have to work on is our ability to communicate. In time, your son will learn to share himself with the people who love him."

"Zachary couldn't have chosen a more perfect wife. I was afraid of his losing you. We love you, Casey."

"I love you too. Now take that nap. Swimming is physical therapy for Zach, and I have to make certain he doesn't get lazy. I'll wake you for dinner. I thought maybe a picnic. After all, we've got perfect weather for it."

"Thank You, God," Zach whispered as he got to his feet and moved toward the porch steps. For the first time in weeks, Zach felt renewed confidence of her love for him.

❧

Casey slid the plate of steaks onto the countertop and removed a pot of boiled potatoes from the burner.

"Potato salad with steak?" Zach asked.

"It's a picnic. I'm making garden salad too."

"Hey, you two," Stacey called, catching their attention when she raced into the kitchen. "You'll never guess what I brought with me."

Casey eyed Zach and both shook their heads. With Stacey there was no telling.

"Fireworks!" Stacey exclaimed, the excitement fading away at Casey's disapproval. "I forgot." She tilted her head toward her sister and derided, "Ms. Safety First."

"One of us has to be," Casey defended.

"It's not like I expect you to light them. Besides, I only brought a couple of rockets and some little firecrackers."

Hopeless, Casey thought, shaking her head at her sister's reasoning. "They're dangerous. I've seen the victims, and let me tell you, it's not a pretty sight."

"You didn't stick a smoke or stink bomb in there, did you?" Zach asked in an effort to diffuse the escalating argument.

"I'll put you in charge of the display so you can see," Stacey said with a huge grin.

"Zach, I don't think you should—"

"Don't worry, sweetheart. We'll be careful. Now let's get this celebration under way. Grab that plate," he told Stacey. "I'll take the potato salad."

From the questioning looks Zach kept throwing her way during dinner, Casey knew he was wondering if she would change her mind. She smiled and winked at him and the electric blue eyes brightened as though a zillion volts charged through them.

Zach held out his plate. "Can I have more potato salad?"

"With steak?" Casey mocked, spooning another serving onto the plate. "Eat your salad."

She grinned when he mouthed, "Yes, Mother" at her.

"Perhaps I should invite your mother to extend her stay," she whispered in his ear minutes later as they cleared the table. "Just long enough for you to learn the difference."

"And if I told you I already know the difference?" he asked. He dropped onto the bench and pulled her into his lap, kissing her softly.

"I guess we can manage without her. Now help my sister before she blows herself up or the mosquitoes tote us away."

The loud bang of the fireworks seemed thunderous in the quiet evening, their brilliance spreading over the darkened sky.

"So much for the fishing," Casey said. "Poor things are probably scared out of their gills by now."

Stacey sighed at the brilliant flash of color. "There's nothing prettier."

"What inspired you to bring fireworks this weekend?"

"They're nothing compared to what's going to happen between you and Zach," Stacey teased.

Casey giggled and snaked an arm about Stacey's neck. A gigantic boom launched the last rocket high into the sky over the lake in bursts of brilliant rays.

They straggled back to the house. Stacey insisted they each

have a sparkler and danced on ahead with her own, leaving a glittery trail of light in the darkness.

Zach waved the glowing object in his hand as he walked. "I loved these things as a kid. Remember what a treat it was when you got an entire box?"

Casey smiled into the darkness. "I was afraid to light them. Thought the sparks would burn me. Watch out," she called when he stumbled on the deck boards.

"My protector," he murmured, giving her a quick kiss.

The evening had flown by, giving Casey little time to analyze her decision. She stepped from the shower and patted herself dry, rubbing the towel over her hair. Maybe that was good, she decided as she pulled on her robe.

Zach lay with his back propped against the headboard and watched Casey blow-dry her hair at the vanity in the bathroom. "I thought we might never share this bed again."

"I promised you'd have your answer this weekend." As Casey turned the dryer off and placed it on the counter, a small box caught her eye. She swallowed hard, rubbing her arms to ward off the frightening chill that encompassed her. Zach couldn't know she'd stopped taking birth control right after he left. It had been her own act of rebellion.

And she would have told him. Wouldn't she? Perspiration beaded at the sudden doubt that overwhelmed her. *No,* she vowed firmly. *I would never trick him into giving me a child, no matter how desperately I want one.*

"I see you came prepared."

Zach jumped from the bed. "Casey, let me explain. I hoped . . .well, prayed, but please understand. We have to take precautions."

Casey shoved her hands into her pockets to keep from wringing them in frustration. "I'm not using anything, Zach. When you left, there was no reason to bother."

He sat on the edge of the bed, his back to her. "Were you going to tell me?"

"I'd never do that to you," Casey whispered. "It's a difficult time for us both. We may want different things, but I agreed to wait. I want your happiness too." One hand slipped over his shoulder. "Today, thinking of being in your arms brings. . . My fantasy, my dream was coming true. I blocked out the reality. Until I saw that box just now. The practical me says you're being protective; the emotional me feels you don't trust me."

"We can't take chances."

"I know why you say we can't, but I've been doing some research of my own," she said. "Your parents have shelves of books on diabetes."

"Probably bought them after I was diagnosed."

She nodded. "One said a child with only one type I diabetic parent has a two to ten percent chance of developing the disease. Those odds sound incredibly good."

"Those odds aren't good enough."

Casey sat down, momentarily rebuffed. "Even if you and every other known diabetic never had children, you couldn't eliminate the disease. There are too many factors."

"I know that," Zach sighed. "But I can't get beyond this fear that what happened to that child could happen to ours."

"So I divorce you, get myself another man, and our child develops diabetes, what have I gained?"

His pained look told Casey he didn't like the idea.

"In the same vein, we have a child, it never develops diabetes, but maybe some other disease or genetic defect. If you were guaranteed the child would not have diabetes, would you be willing to risk the others?"

"Casey, you're being too blasé about this."

"No, I'm being realistic. Hiding behind fear does not make

it go away, Zach. You're a pediatrician. You've treated children every day. Some with minor ailments—colds, sore throats, others with more serious problems—physical defects, incurable illnesses. They were all very resilient, eager to get on with life. Do you think that child was any different?"

"His mother will never forgive herself. She thought he had the flu. Kept giving him orange juice. He was in a coma when he arrived at the hospital."

"Would you feel differently if he were alive today?"

"I don't know. No, maybe I do. Maybe we would blindly have followed our hearts and a little one would be on the way."

The heaviness of her heart expressed itself in Casey's sigh. "Another lesson in life well learned." The words had a sarcastic ring, as the hopelessness suddenly seemed overpowering.

"We can't have a child," Zach insisted. "Not until we can be sure."

"The unknown entity is always difficult to face," Casey said softly, "but life's about what God wants for us. We don't make the decisions and even if we can't always understand them, God does. I've nursed those kids at the hospital, and if nothing else, their joy for living is what gives everyone else hope."

"Where does this leave us, Casey? I love you and I don't think I could bear losing you."

The anguish in his eyes matched the feeling in her heart as she slid into his arms. "I think we both need to let God take control of our problems, Zach. Only He knows what He intends for us. We can set the goals, but His will is the only one that matters. Right now, before we take this step, we need to pray together. Will you start?"

Accepting the hand he held toward her, she bowed her head and closed her eyes.

"Heavenly Father, we come to You tonight. . ."

His words trailed off, making it obvious that he wasn't comfortable.

"Seeking Your guidance," Casey prompted softly.

He started again and soon his voice strengthened and the words poured forth. He beseeched God to help him set aside his fears, to be the husband she deserved, and to set forth the path they should follow.

His prayer was so detailed that by closing all Casey could add was a heartfelt "Amen" before leaning into his arms.

The warmth comforted her, pushing the doubts into the recesses of her mind, replacing them with pleasure. This was where she wanted to be. "I understand, Zach. I really do. I also know tonight has to be a new beginning for us both."

Watery moonlight streamed through the window, highlighting the planes of his face as Zach's lips covered hers.

The missing bits of her life tumbled into place as reality replaced the dreams that had kept her going through the rough period.

☙

Casey flashed her husband a cheeky grin. There was something exhilarating about sitting in the front of the boat, the wind whipping hair and clothing, the spray of water misting her warm skin. Then maybe it had more to do with the intense state of happiness she had felt upon awakening in Zach's arms.

"You still enjoy this," Zach called as he lifted himself up and stared at her over the protective shield of the divided window.

"I love all the things we do together," she shouted back. "The only thing missing is a child."

"Casey." Her name came out sounding like a groan.

She walked back to take the seat opposite him. "So where do we go from here?"

Zach brought the boat to a halt in the middle of the lake and they rocked slightly with the movement of the water. "I asked that last night."

"You asked where you stood," Casey corrected. "I'm asking what we should do about our conflicting opinions."

"I wish I could explain this fear. Sometimes I feel it's totally irrational, but I don't think I'm being selfish."

"What about genetic counseling? Have you ruled that out?"

"What if my beliefs are valid?" he countered. "Will we still have a marriage if you can't have a child?"

"There are other ways of being a parent. Are you open to adoption?"

"Let me think."

"Give yourself a chance, Zach. I think your research will help you realize life is for living. Not hiding."

seven

"My respect for your sister grows every day," Zach said as Stacey's car drove away. "How did she convince Mom to leave at the crack of dawn?"

"Dawn? It's nine-thirty," Casey said. "Stacey claimed pressing engagements. And even a mother wouldn't intrude on a second honeymoon."

"Thank heaven for that." Zach gathered Casey in his arms, the last words smothered as she raised up to meet his kiss. "Put on your swimsuit," he whispered. "And some suntan oil. I'm taking you fishing."

Casey sighed in a mock swoon. "How romantic. The bugs will eat me alive."

"Use repellent."

"They'll stick in the oil," Casey argued as they crossed the porch. Oh, why not? She liked fishing. "Okay. If you agree to a small contest."

"Which is?"

"Biggest catch keeps that person from cooking tonight."

"You're on."

Casey changed in a flash, the slap of her flip-flops echoing through the quiet house. She stepped onto the porch and took a deep breath. Peace was such a tangible thing at Solitude. Almost touchable, or maybe the privacy wrapped her in a protective bunting. They never seemed to have any at home with the phone, Zach's pager, their work, and the friends who often dropped by to visit. The pressures of the outside world didn't seem to follow them here.

Zach came around the house carrying a set of oars. "Race you to the boat."

"No." Her sharp response stopped him in his tracks.

When he would have objected, Zach smiled a slow, easy smile. "You're right. I keep testing myself."

Casey's hand closed about his arm. "What are those for?"

"The one-man boat."

"I thought we were fishing off the pier. I should have known. Do you think we can manage it without drowning?"

"We've done it before. Remember?"

Their gazes met, and they shared a smile. The first time had been on their honeymoon when he'd wanted to go fishing, and she'd refused to let him out of her sight.

"Very well," Casey agreed with raised brows.

Zach kissed her, his lips lingering.

"The boat, my darling," Casey said, providing the necessary encouragement.

"You first," Zach said as he untied the one-man boat from the post near the boat ramp.

"No, you."

"My knee's hardly bothering me today."

"Would you just get in the boat?"

"How long are you going to keep this up?" Zach grumbled as he negotiated his way to the seat.

Casey slipped off her cover-up and threw it over the side, wading out into the water. "Don't start with me. That macho image doesn't cut it when I know what could happen."

"Okay. Can I at least maneuver us out into the lake?"

"Last I heard your arms worked fine." The boat tilted dangerously as she climbed in. Casey moved carefully in the limited space, spreading her towel and then applying suntan lotion to her arms and legs before reaching for the insect repellent. Her nose wrinkled as she sprayed it generously over her exposed skin. "I hope I don't have a reaction."

Without looking up, Casey felt his intent regard. Her body responded and she focused on the water, watching the ripples spread. The sound of the oars dipping into the lake made their aloneness so much more poignant. "This is isolated."

"We prefer private, Casey. No one here but us and the wildlife." A frog croaked and jumped from a nearby log as if to prove his point. "Hey, don't rock the boat."

The silence stretched around them as the oars bumped against the boat, and Zach baited the fishing rods.

"Hey, that's mine," she cried when he cast far out into the water with a casual flick of the wrist. The ease with which he performed the task drove her crazy. Casey had made a special trip to the tackle store before their last weekend excursion to purchase the rod and reel. The store clerk assured her she would be able to cast with ease. It hadn't worked. She'd managed to tangle the line and snag herself.

Zach passed her the rod. "Here you go."

Minutes seemed more like hours, as neither of them had so much as a nibble.

"Those firecrackers scared all the fish away. Perhaps we should move. . ." Casey's words trailed off as she found it too easy to get lost in the way his gaze kept drifting back to her.

The air electrified, almost as if a thunderstorm were fast approaching, and for a moment she considered jumping into the lake to cool off.

"Come over here." The intensity of his stare made the blue eyes softer. A tiny smile touched the corner of his mouth.

Casey flirted with him. "But you said to be still."

"And you never listen to what I tell you."

"Right," she exclaimed with a burst of laughter as she moved slowly toward him, rocking the boat.

"Easy," Zach called breathlessly as he grabbed the sides.

His arms wrapped about her tiny midriff, and she relaxed, sinking into his cushioning embrace before his lips searched hers out and shattered all remaining calm.

Casey held him tightly, unsure of the source of the crazy rocking. "We're going to turn this boat over," she moaned as the vessel dipped a little further to one side.

"Not if we're careful." His arms encircled her, one hand smoothing the small of her back as his lips all but singed hers.

She turned toward him. "Casey, be careful," Zach warned, too late as their movement tilted the boat and dropped them into the depths of the cold water. Still they held each other, the buoyancy keeping them afloat.

"Ugh! What is that?" Casey shrilled as she groped between their bodies. She moaned when she removed the slimy fish caught in their human net.

Zach laughed heartily as he took the still flailing fish and tossed it back into the water.

"Why did you do that?" Casey wailed. "It's the first one we caught all day."

"And I'd highly recommend the method," Zach teased, bringing a deeper flush to her skin, "but I couldn't eat a fish that had been familiar with us."

"Oh you," Casey said, slapping water toward him before she swam away. "Now we'll have to start all over."

"And maybe this time we'll get it right."

"Or keep practicing until we do," she agreed, her smile rivaling the sun.

❧

She is so perfect, Zach thought that night as he held Casey close. "Is it my imagination or have you gained a few pounds?"

"I lost a few after you left, and then they came back and brought friends. I've been eating everything in sight."

Zach sat up in the bed. "You couldn't be. . ."

"What?" she murmured drowsily.

"Pregnant?"

Suddenly wide awake, Casey's mind whirled with his question. He was really obsessed by this. "I considered it when I missed my cycle, but the test came out negative."

He lay back and rested an arm over his eyes. "That would be payback after what I did to you."

"What do you mean by that?"

He groaned. "Just that I was trying to protect you by leaving."

A deeper chasm rent Casey's heart. Where had his objectivity gone? How would she ever convince him to look at the broader picture? "I figure stress and poor eating habits are the culprits. I've downed enough junk food lately."

"Why didn't you go in for an exam?"

"I didn't want anybody else to know. Not even Stacey. I did the test while I was in San Francisco." She sighed drowsily as he kissed her neck.

"I'm sorry. Forgive me?"

Casey adjusted her head against his shoulder and felt him tremble as her fingers pressed ever so lightly against his skin. "Get some rest. You're not totally recovered and I need sleep. We have tomorrow."

"Promise?" he asked.

"Yes. Tell me a bedtime story about the house we're going to buy."

"I'm not sure one house will meet all your demands. Let's see, spiraling staircase, widow's walk, floor-length windows, and of course, rope braid trim everywhere," Zach recited. "Did I miss anything?"

"Only the most important thing. We have to have a carved tester bed for the front chamber."

"For us, I hope?"

"Of course. Our guests can sleep in ordinary beds."

"Of course. And don't forget the. . ."

"Pocket doors," Casey exclaimed in unison with him. "I almost forgot them."

"Too bad the Bellamy Mansion's not for sale. Maybe we should build our own version of a plantation. I heard that bed-and-breakfast you love so much is for sale."

"And just where did you plan to find a million dollars? I'll settle for something a little less grand, thank you."

"No settling for us. Our house is going to be a showplace."

"We're not going to have enough furniture for a larger house. I wonder if I can talk Mom and Dad into an early inheritance?"

"Please, no. We'd start World War III."

"Then you'll have to help me find more."

Zach rolled his eyes, a contented smile lurking around the corners of his mouth as he reached for the lamp switch.

☙

Casey lay, wide awake, listening to the sound of Zach's steady breathing. She felt more loved than she dreamed possible. Everything seemed perfect, on the surface. She didn't fool herself, though. His renewed commitment had negative as well as positive aspects. His suspicious reaction to the possibility of pregnancy struck her as very negative.

Casey's tongue slipped out to wet her dry lips at the thought. How would he react to knowing the thrill she felt when she thought she might be expecting his child? Her grief reinforced itself with the negative test result. Not only had she lost Zach, but also her hope for the future.

She eased from the bed and grabbed a shirt from the chair. It was Zach's, a sport shirt smelling of his clean male scent. A glance over her shoulder assured her he was still asleep.

In the kitchen, Casey combined the ingredients for a shake, hesitating before she turned on the handheld stirrer. A couple of minutes wouldn't wake him. Casey picked up the glass and moved to the sofa. She settled in and took a sip of the drink.

What were they going to do? Twice now, she'd witnessed Zach's negative reaction to the possibility of a child in their future. The first time when he failed to trust her, and now when her being pregnant would have been punishment from God for his wrong.

They were both wearing rose-colored glasses, pushing aside the negative as they reached for the positive. How long did he expect her to do that? Until her childbearing years were past and it was no longer a problem? Casey refused to accept that choice. She wanted children now while she was young enough to enjoy them.

Her marriage vows were a lifelong commitment. Not something to forsake the moment the pathway got a little rough.

Where could they find the answers? Her gaze rested on the Promise Book lying on the coffee table. She'd read a bit, just until she was drowsy. Two verses penned inside the front cover caught her attention: Psalm 46:1, "God is our refuge and strength, a very present help in trouble," and 1 Corinthians 6:20, "For you were bought at a price; therefore glorify God in your body and in your spirit, which are God's."

The book dropped to her lap. "Lord, what are Your plans for us? We accept that the price of our salvation was Your Son, that Your grace is all we need to be accepted in Your kingdom. Are we looking so deep inside ourselves that we're missing what You would have for us?"

The lamp's light pooled about her as she settled on the end of the sofa and opened the book to the marker. For the next hour, she read verse after verse on the various topics, and it seemed as if each one were handpicked to speak to her heart. Casey and Zach hadn't been to church since coming to

Solitude. Casey missed the message and fellowship of their own Grace Church.

Totally engrossed, she suddenly felt the hairs on the back of her neck prickle. She scanned the windows. Nothing. Her eyes dropped to the page again.

"Casey?"

She dropped the book with a little scream before flashing him a sheepish look.

Zach hesitated in the bedroom doorway, blinking his sleep-heavy eyes as he focused on her. "Why didn't you wake me?"

"Why should you be awake because I couldn't sleep? I was thirsty, and then I saw this."

He rubbed a hand over his eyes and yawned. "What time is it?"

She shrugged. "Are you hungry?"

"I'll make myself a sandwich. What about you?"

"I'm fine. This book of scriptures is wonderful."

Casey lifted the book so he could read the title. Zach nodded. "Mom gave it to me when I was diagnosed."

"I can't put it down. My couple of minutes turned into an hour."

Zach removed the twist tie from the bread bag and laid two slices out a plate. "You plan to finish tonight?"

"Just to the end of this section."

"How about some music?"

"Too distracting," she murmured, her eyes never leaving his face.

"Talk?" Zach asked as he wandered even closer.

"Too distracting," Casey repeated with a knowing grin.

"Me?" Zach asked as he dropped over the back of the sofa and slipped his arms about her.

"Definitely too distracting," she said as their lips met and clung.

❧

Zach watched as Casey stirred on the bed beside him, still asleep from their late night. He was tired himself. She had told him to come back to bed, suggesting he bring his sandwich. Their lighthearted fun began when she filched the sandwich and ran to the opposite side of the room.

He followed, laughing when she jumped onto the bed and stood, rocking from one foot to the other as she waited for him to make his move. He rolled across the bed and found himself alone as she jumped to safety. A furious pillow fight ensued, Casey unable to wield any impact as she giggled like a schoolgirl. After their play, they had curled up together and talked for hours.

Getting back into a routine was going to be difficult. Their time at Solitude was coming to an end and no matter how hard he tried to hold on to the good times, Zach worried about how they were going to cope once they returned home.

Casey hadn't mentioned a baby again, but he knew a child was never far from her thoughts. At times he'd catch her deep in thought, and when he offered the traditional penny, she claimed her thoughts were worth more. It was the same with the baby commercials on television. She always beamed, sometimes laughing, others sighing as she watched them. How would she cope with never becoming a mother?

"Good morning," she said, rolling toward him as she woke.

"Same to you, sleepyhead." Zach leaned over to kiss her. "What time did you finally go to sleep?"

Her wide yawn verified she was still half-asleep. "Around three-thirty."

"What if I mix your bran shake and then you catch more shut-eye while I swim?"

"Breakfast in bed? You are a sweetie."

"A keeper?"

Zach found himself unable to do anything more than grin like an idiot in response to her smile as Casey wrapped her arms around his neck. "I think so," she mumbled almost incoherently.

"You asleep, Casey?" he murmured a few seconds later when she grew very still.

"Almost. Forget the shake, but I'm trusting you to swim for at least thirty minutes."

His lips touched hers briefly. "Sweet dreams."

꙳

More than thirty minutes had passed, Casey conceded hours later as she kicked her feet against the sheet and pushed it to the side. She glanced toward the expanse of glass that served as a wall, Solitude its pictorial subject.

Suddenly, she felt like singing. Instead she slipped her legs over the side of the bed and stood. Zach was probably very impatient, having finished his swim long ago. Of course, she didn't really feel like swimming, the inertia an effect of her late night.

The reflection in the cheval mirror caught her eye. Casey ran a hand over her stomach. Zach was right. She was putting on weight. Maybe a lap or two wouldn't hurt after all.

After pulling on a vivid orange one-piece swimsuit, she made a side trip by the storage shed. The bulky floats made the pool chair heavier than she thought, Casey decided, wearing it on her shoulders like a large hat.

Zach swiped water from his eyes and frowned. "I thought we agreed to call Jake to get that thing out here."

Casey dropped the length of nylon rope on the pier. Once she got the chair into the lake, she'd anchor it to the pier and use it as a float after her swim. "I've moved heavier stuff at the shop," she said.

Her arms refused to synchronize the movement, one going

up while the other bent at the elbow. The extra weight carried her forward, flying with the chair toward the lake. The resounding splash sent water everywhere, the wave blinding Zach.

"Casey!" he yelled, sounding panic-stricken when she disappeared from view.

She spluttered as she came up, sweeping the water-slicked hair from her eyes. "Get the chair."

"Forget the chair. Are you okay? Did you hurt yourself?"

"I'm perfectly fine," Casey argued before she swam off to retrieve the chair. She'd gone to too much trouble to lose it now.

"Let me," Zach said as he swam past. "I can't believe you sometimes. That thing weighs at least half as much as you do."

"Hold it there," Casey said as she scrambled onto the pier for the rope. She tied off her end and tossed it to him before diving back into the water.

"Seems like an awful lot of trouble for nothing," he grumbled, not quite able to hide his smile in response to hers.

"Aren't you a prune yet?" Casey demanded. "How long have you been swimming? You know you aren't supposed to overdo."

"Easy, sweetheart. I'd just jumped in before you started the one-woman stunt show. As ordered, I swam for a half hour and then fell asleep in the sunshine."

Casey moved her fingers to his jaw. "Why didn't you come back to bed?"

Zach shook his head, laughing as the water flew from his thick curls and splattered her like a wet dog. "Too wet. I missed you though."

Their water-soaked lips sizzled as they made contact, their heads slipping under the water when they forgot where they were.

"Enough of that," she declared as they broke the surface. "I've got to swim. All this lazing is putting the pounds on."

"Let's work them off."

Casey scooped a handful of water into his face and broke free, swimming off as quickly as a sleek seal.

"Hey," Zach yelled after her. "This isn't what I had in mind."

"You spend too much time thinking." She went under and resurfaced, watching Zach advance. Casey dodged to one side and then the other before he grabbed her about the waist and flung her back into the water. Her laughter-filled screams echoed around the lake as Zach dunked, splashed, and then demanded a game of water tag.

"Enough," Casey yelled as she projected herself onto the chair.

Zach followed, the chair plunging forward when he rested his hands on the front of the arms. "Not yet. I owe you for that last dunking."

"Oh, give me a break! I had to climb up onto your shoulders and jump to get you under once."

"You almost drowned me." Zach's lips feather-touched hers with tantalizing persuasion. "I love you, Casey."

"I love you too."

No further words were needed to express the deep love that showed in their eyes. Casey reached out and touched his face. "Why don't you get a float?"

After he disappeared, she swished her fingers through the water. As usual, her idle thoughts transgressed quickly from the deep love for her husband to her enjoyment of the place and togetherness to wondering what Zach had been like as a boy.

A large plastic float glided overhead and bounced on the water. Casey grabbed the rope and held on as she waited for him to join her. "Tell me about your childhood here."

Zach dived in and climbed onto the float. "A loner. There were never many kids around. Mom usually invited one of my friends for two weeks every summer. Said she couldn't handle more. I pretty much kept myself occupied until I started noticing girls. That's when I told Mom I didn't want to come here for the summer any more.

"She seemed real upset, so I gave in. Then Dad decided I should work at the insurance company with him. Said I needed to learn how to earn a dollar. Mom never came alone. I used to bring my dates and friends out on the weekends."

"So I could have married an insurance salesman?"

"No. I'd pretty much decided I was going to be a doctor. I'd discussed it with the guidance counselor and took all the right courses. Kept my grades up too."

"Bet that was tough for a Romeo like you."

Zach swatted a handful of water in Casey's direction. "Fairly," he agreed with a wink.

She retaliated, kicking her feet vigorously in the water and then laughing as he fell off the float with a mighty splash. "Mom and Dad took us on buying trips sometimes. Stacey hated them. I had this dream of making a rare find. They had their hands full teaching me how to bargain. I always wanted to pay asking price. I made some junk buys at first, but I think they're proud of my ability now."

He hugged the float to his chest and treaded water. "Would you like to be an antique dealer, Casey?"

"You sound surprised."

"I knew you were really into it as a hobby but I'd never dreamed. . . I had no idea you were that serious."

"In the back of my mind, I thought that one day, after the children were in school, I might pursue the business either full- or part-time. I turned it into a hobby because I didn't want Mom and Dad feeling obligated to include me on the buying trips."

"You didn't have to travel. There were other ways."

Casey shrugged. "Nursing isn't that bad. You and I got to work together at times."

"My leaving must have caused a lot of strain for you at the hospital."

Casey didn't dispute the truth of his statement. "Things were awkward. Some people didn't know what to say. After a while, they realized I didn't expect them to say anything. Others were curious and used concern as their guise. I knew they were looking for information for the grapevine. Some of the things that got back to me were pretty disturbing."

"I'm sorry."

"I know." Her hand slipped into his. "I'm sorry too, but we're going to be okay."

Zach squeezed her hand tighter and his smile brought an immediate softening to his features. Their time apart had been difficult for them both, Casey realized. She stayed and faced the world while he ran, but he hadn't been excluded from the pain. He'd been in his own private nightmare—a bad dream where he would remain until he accepted he couldn't control his life, until he put God back in control of his choices.

They idled away a good part of the day in the lake before hunger forced them inside. "What about a film festival?" Zach suggested as they walked toward the house. "I know you prefer the big screen, but we could pick up some tapes."

His arm rested about Casey's shoulder and he moved easily. Soon it would be difficult to discern any injury.

"Only if we buy popcorn."

"To go."

"And then tomorrow I want a picnic in the woods. I'd hate to have lugged that hamper up here for nothing."

"Who's going to carry it? With my bad knee I know you wouldn't want—"

"I can see your knee is going to come in handy in the future. No problem. There's a couple of backpacks that will hold just enough for a picnic."

"Just so long as we don't forget the blanket. I always did love picnicking with you," Zach said as he pulled the screen door open.

"It's because you like my potato salad. Since we're going for some tapes, what about plundering around a couple of shops?"

"You always liked to chat with that old fellow who has the barn."

"Sounds perfect."

❧

Casey glanced at Zach as she parked their SUV in front of the one-time tobacco packinghouse. How did he really feel about these excursions? She'd dragged him on so many. He bore up well, uncomplaining, often finding things of interest at the shops and estate auctions.

"Sure you're up to this?"

"It'll be fun."

"Trying to convince yourself?"

"Stop analyzing my every word, Casey." The brief command was accompanied by a look of pure exasperation. "Let's see what this place has to offer. Who knows, maybe he's got that rare find you mentioned earlier."

The building was packed to the rafters with just about everything, the proprietor knowledgeable and more than happy to talk shop with another antique lover.

Casey half listened as the man gave her the history on a carved fireplace mantel she admired, her gaze drifting across the room to where Zach examined an old iron. She almost laughed as he gauged the weight by hefting the item a few times.

"Once refinished, the mantel would be a real conversation piece, don't you think, Mrs. Taylor?"

"I'm sorry," she said upon realizing he was waiting for a response.

"This piece," he repeated, running a gnarled hand gently over the carved wood. "A real conversation starter."

"Definitely. It has a look that can't be duplicated."

"Casey," Zach called. "Come look."

"Excuse me."

"Is that what I think?" he asked, pointing out a patch of silver paint.

"Oh yes. Just like the one at Solitude," she demanded as she tried to squeeze closer.

"Found something?"

"She loves those old antique tubs."

The man nodded. "Lot of people looking for them now. For a while they were throwing them out right and left. Replacing them with those newfangled fiberglass jobs. Got some washstands somewhere."

Impulsively, Casey looked at Zach when the old man turned away. "Buy it for me."

"You haggle with him. You're better at it."

"No, you," she whispered.

Casey watched as the men went back and forth on the price, finally settling closer to the dealer's offer than Zach's.

"I tried," Zach told her as they walked toward the truck after making arrangements for the man to hold the tub until they could have it picked up.

"You did great. I'd probably have ended up paying full price. I bought you something too."

His eyes lit at the prospect of a present. "What?"

"Close your eyes and hold out your hand."

Zach did, his fingers closing quickly around the heavy iron she rested on his palm. "I'd have bought a set if he'd had another." He eyed the battered relic and waited for the punch line. "You always wanted weights."

"You know me too well."

"Not yet," Casey teased, kissing him before she started the truck, "but we've got a lifetime to sort out the particulars."

eight

Casey's body swayed in time with the music on the radio as she spread mustard over a slice of bread. She enjoyed the warm breeze drifting through the open window. The soft blue, cotton ball cloud-laden sky confirmed it was a beautiful day for a picnic.

The screen door slammed, and she smiled at Zach as he moved around the corner of the cabinet. The towel slung about his shoulders caught the rivulets of water streaming down his neck. He searched the cabinets, banging the last door shut and murmuring, "Too bad."

Intrigued, Casey asked, "What are you looking for?"

"No container for the bran shakes."

Casey bounced a marshmallow off his chest. "I can see you're really broken up about that. It's peanut butter sandwiches and nothing to drink for you."

"Something, please. Water. Even the shake," he pleaded.

"It just so happens I thought of that yesterday." She opened the refrigerator and set out a wedge of cheese along with apples and grapes. "And these." Casey added cardboard cartons to the collection.

"Grape juice?"

"There's apple if you prefer."

Zach groaned. "Has anyone died from being too healthy?"

"You're the one interested in research," she countered.

"Ha. Ha. Can I at least carry the hamper?"

Casey shook her head. "Too bulky. We can divide the lot into the backpacks. You can carry the blanket."

"That wool thing?"

She grinned. "Get dressed, Zach. And don't forget—"

"The brace. I know." His defeated response changed as he slipped his hands over Casey's shoulders. "At least kiss me good morning."

She grabbed the towel and pulled his head downward. "Have I told you how much I love you?"

He murmured, "Let's forget the picnic."

"Nope, it's already the plan."

"Plans don't always get carried through. A little spontaneity never hurt."

"That can't be Dr. Taylor talking. 'Not now, Casey,' " she mimicked, " 'I've got an office full of patients waiting.' 'I'm too tired.' Oh, and lest we forget, 'I'd love to meet you for lunch, darling, but I've got to run over to the hospital.' I'd given up hope of ever developing any feminine wiles."

"What if I agree to devote less time to work and more to you? Say, starting now."

His mischievous smile captured her attention, but Casey said, "Good idea. Meet me on the porch in ten minutes."

His deep chuckle filled the room. Casey divided their lunch into the packs and zipped them shut, listening to him move about the bedroom.

"You'll suffocate in those jeans," she warned when he came out tucking his shirt into his pants.

He gave her bare legs the once-over. "And you'll probably end up with poison ivy."

"You think so? Maybe I should change."

He caught her arm as she started toward the bedroom. "Nah. Just walk in front so I can enjoy the view."

Casey wrinkled her nose at him. Zach grabbed the backpacks and followed, resting them on the porch long enough to do a couple of stretches.

"Nice day," she murmured.

"Beautiful view," he agreed.

Casey flushed as she straightened and looked at him. "I was talking about the weather."

"Perfect weather," Zach agreed, grinning as he helped Casey on with the pack. "Not one rainy day. Got enough food in these for the ants?"

"Cozy, rainy days get a bad rap," she said, ignoring his jibe. "How's the knee?"

"A twinge or two. The walk will work them out. Don't worry," Zach said as uncertainty flared in Casey's eyes. "I know. We stop when I say so."

"You're learning."

The path wound through Solitude, the lake never more than a few feet away. Casey skirted any suspicious looking greenery and asked, "Where are we headed?"

"The waterfall." Zach spoke of the place he knew to be Casey's favorite. "Mom had Jake plant wildflowers there. I can't wait to see how it turned out."

"It was paradise even without flowers. In fact, all of Solitude is magnificent. I hate to think about leaving."

"Don't look so woebegone. We'll come back," Zach promised, his hand closing about hers.

"I can't help but wonder when. With you working day and night on your research, and me working night shift and spending time at the store, we'll barely see each other."

"I'll work extra hard so we can have the same days off. And I'll have an office at home. Close enough for you to practice your feminine wiles."

Her laughter trilled about them. "More like close enough for me to drag you out when you try to work even harder. At least you'll be handy when I have research results to discuss."

They walked on, neither saying anything as they moved in

single file when the path narrowed, and then side by side when it widened.

Finally, in desperation, Casey spoke. "You realize we have to talk about these feelings you're experiencing?"

The familiar mask descended once again. "Yes," Zach admitted finally. "I keep waiting for the right time, but I suspect later won't be any different from now."

Pleasure momentarily overshadowed her confusion as they broke through a clearing. Casey had discovered the spot during her honeymoon rambling. Zach teased that he should have taken her to Niagara Falls when she kept raving about its beauty.

Though man-made, the natural look of the waterfall had withstood the tests of time. Then again, it had been there since the first Taylors started creating their private retreat, making it far from new.

When Zach attempted to explain the mechanics of how they rerouted the water from the lake, Casey refused to listen, wanting no interference from reality when it came to her romantic illusions. She didn't care how it worked—just that it did.

She pushed the straps of the backpack off and relinquished the load to Zach as she rubbed her shoulders.

Zach held up the blanket. "Where do you want this?"

Casey wandered a bit, coming to a halt in a spot with a view of the waterfall and the colorful burst of wildflowers. "Here."

The blanket floated through the air, and she caught the edges, bending to smooth it over the grass before settling on one corner. Casey rocked to one side and flicked the fabric aside, feeling for and finding a small rock.

"I'll take care of that for you, princess." Zach skipped the rock across the water. There was a plop, and rings circled the area where it hit. He moved the backpacks and lowered himself carefully onto the ground, stretching his legs out before him.

One hand massaged his knee. "Did you remember what day it is?"

Casey stopped digging in the bags, a faintly eager look flashing into the eyes that met his. "I wondered if you would."

Zach captured her hand. "Our first anniversary. No romantic dinners for us," he added somewhat regretfully.

"Wrong," Casey said, indicating the food they had brought along. "It doesn't have to be a five-star restaurant with candles to be romantic."

"There's something I want you to have." Zach shifted, slipping a hand briefly into his jeans pocket. The diamonds in the eternity band he held between his fingers sparkled like prisms in the sunlight. "Some say these rings are for when you've been married a long time. I'd rather it be my promise to you that our marriage will last an eternity."

Tears glimmered in her eyes as Casey stared down at the ring and back at her husband. "I didn't get you anything."

"Sure you did." He smiled at her puzzled look. "The iron."

"That was a joke."

Pleasure softened his reserved expression. "You gave me a gift that can't be bought. To me, a second chance is more precious than anything else in the world."

Casey flung her arms about him, almost unbalancing them both as she laughed and then cried with joy. Zach held her in the circle of his arms, a comfortable silence enclosing them as they admired the ring.

His head suddenly lifted from the curve of her shoulder. "I wonder if there's a way to make you understand the things that fill my mind."

"I want to."

Her earnest admission didn't surprise Zach. "I know you do. But first you need to understand I'm afraid for us. For any children we might have."

"The diabetes?"

"Partially," he agreed, an unexpected somberness overtaking him. "Then there's the little voice that insists I get out of your life before I hurt you."

"Zach?" Casey whispered, laying a hand on his arm.

The distance that separated them became light years as he drifted into the past. "I've never experienced anything like that day. It scared me," he admitted. "I hadn't slept much the night before. Rushed out of the house without breakfast, no time for lunch, and then that case came into the ER." His eyes seemed to overflow with sorrow. "The mother was a petite, dark-haired woman. Very much like you. I can't forget the way she crumpled when I told her the boy was dead. I caught her before she fell, and she just held on. You could tell her world had been destroyed. The one thought that kept running through my head was 'This could be Casey.' "

"But it wasn't."

"It could have been," he insisted. "That child's death was like someone turned on a light. If we'd met in high school, chances are we'd have had half a dozen kids by now." The corner of his mouth lifted with wry amusement. "Possibly two, if I'd still been in residency. Strange how your perspective changes as you grow older. Certain things become more valuable, almost precious.

"Our time together is limited. I can't help but think our togetherness would be lost completely if we have a child. Call me insecure, possessive. I can't help what I feel. I'm human. I've only had you in my life for such a short time. But I was prepared to give you a child because it was what you wanted."

"You could have told me you weren't ready."

"I didn't know," Zach exclaimed. "Every time we discussed children, I actually thought, 'Sure, one day.' Maybe all those thoughts kicked in when that child died, but then I believed I was protecting you. I've seen your heart break when a newborn at the hospital dies. I hurt when you hurt. I know now it was selfish."

Zach adjusted his body on the blanket, propping his hands behind his head as he stared up at the sky. "I keep saying it's fear for you, but I'm afraid too. What kind of father would I make? A diabetic doctor with a full-time practice, always working, too busy to be a decent husband, much less a father.

"Where would I find the energy to help you raise a child? As it is, it's virtually impossible to maintain my own routine. What about long-term complications? I've been diagnosed for twelve years now. Eye disease or diabetic nephropathy? A shortened life span? Is it fair to you to have to raise our child alone? Fair to the child not to have a father?

"And what about the child? Why should he or she be subjected to the frustrations of growing up with the disease? Being denied things other children take for granted?"

Casey leaned toward him, resting a hand against his chest. "Where's the negativity coming from, Zach? Look at the facts. Many people never develop the complications, and those who do have had at least fifteen years of chronic and progressive diabetes. Yours has been neither. Is it fair to deprive the world of a potential genius just because you're afraid?" When he rolled his eyes, she relented, the corners of her mouth dimpling. "Okay, maybe not a genius. You *would* be the father."

"Thanks." He offered her an off-center smile, the flash of humor seeming so out of place with the seriousness of their discussion.

"Diabetes often skips generations."

"It's also the fifth leading cause of disease-related death," he countered. "I know all about subjective interpretations.

I've been there. I've experienced all the stages. Attempted the life of self-control."

Zach sat up and leaned closer. "You know what really scares me? I'm afraid my diabetes will place too much stress on our marriage. What happens if one day you decide you can't take any more?"

"I wasn't looking for an easy out when I married you. That's why I'm giving us another chance. The minister left nothing out of our vows. Divorce is too easy. Making a good marriage better is hard work. Every article on good relationships stresses communication, but no one ever tells us how to get beyond the fear that keeps us from opening up completely, making ourselves vulnerable to another human being. Right now I'm acting strictly on prayer and instinct, believing I've made the right decision. . .hoping we'll make everything right again."

"Your logic makes my actions even stupider."

"Not to me. I have to understand what you want and need."

"Other than you, I don't know what I need anymore," he exclaimed almost angrily. Zach got to his feet and stood staring at the waterfall. "Why does everything have to be so complicated? Never one plus one. Always some sort of human algebra figuring in the xs and ys."

"What's life without complications?"

He turned to face her. "I'd love to find out."

"Everyone has problems, Zach."

"I love you, Casey. I really do. But there are times when I want to mope, and that everlasting optimism of yours drives me up the wall."

"You want me to think like you?" she asked with a choked, desperate laugh. Casey moved to her knees and began gathering the picnic items. "Okay. Let's give up on us. There's no hope. If we get back to the house now, we can be packed and out of here by nightfall."

"Casey?" The sun fought the chilly black silence that enveloped them.

She sank downward and stared at him. "I'm having a hard time with this myself. That optimism you hate is well-disguised panic. You had your experiment with depression. Did it serve any real purpose? Other than confusing you even more?"

"I'd be the first to admit running away wasn't smart."

"This has nothing to do with intelligence, Zach."

"The tendency is inherited. I was one of the unlucky twenty-five percent who developed diabetes before fifty. Who's to say our child wouldn't too?"

"And who says it would? What was the child's diagnosis?"

"Complications from undiagnosed diabetes." He walked off.

Casey rose and followed, feeling the mist from the waterfall as they drew nearer to the comforting sounds of tinkling water.

"It was more than his dying. You've been pushing yourself for months—carrying two patient loads when Donald was out sick—losing sleep to make certain we spent time together. Everyone has limitations.

"Diabetes is a nuisance," she agreed. "Nobody likes the shots, the testing, the strict diet, but like other things, it becomes a part of life. Actually, you're healthier because you're forced to take care of your condition.

"I'm not going to tell you we could have healthy children. You know the odds as well as I do. Nor do I say we'll have a child or this marriage is over. I am asking that you keep an open mind. Help me explore the possibilities and make an educated decision. Is that too much to ask?"

"Not as long as you agree the time is there." He sounded almost desperate. "I have to know that we would be doing the best thing. I couldn't bear to lose you or our child."

"Losing someone is never easy," Casey said, smiling at him as she traced a finger along his jaw. "I don't want to harp on the past because I want to move forward. But when we were apart, there were days when I didn't want to get out of bed, days when I had no purpose for living. I hated feeling that way. At times I hated you for making it happen. Then I realized that no matter how angry I was with you, I still loved you. And I am happy to have you back in my life."

Gathering her close, Zach held her against his body. "I was miserable without you," he said. "I wanted to come home but I couldn't. I think I came pretty close to a nervous breakdown. When I tried to sleep, I had nightmares. I wrote myself a prescription for sleeping pills. I don't remember much after that, except one evening I woke up groggy, wondering where I was and realized I'd lost a day. I knew I had to stop. I let my head convince my heart that what I was doing was in our best interests. I was afraid you'd never forgive me."

"Why didn't you tell me this instead of running out, Zach? I've always told you I wanted children. You never said a word."

He tensed. "It was the most shattering realization. I'm afraid, Casey. The truth could mean I lose you."

"The truth may very well be the only hope we have. Be honest with me, Zach," she pleaded. "Is there any hope for us having a child?"

"The only answer I have for that is I don't know."

Casey fought back the urge to tell him nothing was as important as his love and having him happy and worry-free, but as true as that was, she had to deal with the possibility of never having a child. Zach had mentioned the stages of coming to grips with his disease. They would be no less painful for her if she couldn't be a mother. Casey moved away and dropped to her knees on the blanket. "I can accept that answer.

For now. We'd better eat."

Together, they spread the meal and nibbled at the food.

Zach yawned widely. "I could use a nap."

"Twenty winks and then we head for home."

Casey lay her head against his shoulder and allowed her eyes to drift closed. Thoughts of their discussion lingered until exhaustion won out. Soon she was asleep.

The first drop of rain hit with a plop, and she brushed it away, unable to do the same with the shower that followed.

"No rain," she grumbled as they pulled the blanket over their heads, finding it very little protection. "We should have paid more attention to your knee."

"Lucky for us there's no lightning since these trees are our only shelter. Let's make a run for it."

Casey swept away the water that trailed into her eyes. "Walk," she reminded. "How's your Gene Kelly imitation?"

"It could use some work."

She laughed as they quickly stuffed items into the backpacks and started toward home. After realizing she wouldn't get any wetter, Casey began to enjoy the rain. She removed her shoes and waded through a pool of clear rainwater, coming back to dance around Zach as he moved more slowly.

"Looks like it's set in." A sudden downpour as they dashed for the porch confirmed Zach's dire prediction.

Casey dried his face with the edge of the blanket. "I can just see David's face when I tell him you got pneumonia playing in the rain."

"A long, very hot shower will take care of the problem. On second thought, you go first. Don't give me that 'I'm the nurse' look. How would I explain you having pneumonia to Stacey?" Zach asked as he opened the front door.

"Considering how you love to hog all the hot water, I think that's a wonderful idea," Casey said. "I won't be long."

Later, Casey sat in the glider, watching the rain that continued to fall. At times it dripped from the eaves of the house, others it poured in a steady stream. A cleansing rain, certain to bring a freshness to the air while it revived the landscape and cooled the temperature.

With the silence, she found it difficult to think of anything other than what Zach had told her. *Come on, Casey,* she chided. *You wanted the truth.*

But he was wrong about some things. Her optimism was not eternal. She had to work at keeping an up attitude, particularly after all that had happened lately.

Happiness wasn't difficult to find when you loved the Lord, had a husband and family who loved you, and adored your work, hobbies, and friends. It was much harder now. Zach hadn't even given her half promises when it came to children, and despite her love for him, Casey wasn't sure their marriage was strong enough to withstand this crisis.

What sort of life would she have without children? A childless marriage had never been a consideration—not even when they first discussed a life together. Not until that child had died with diabetic complications.

Casey certainly understood how losing a patient to the same disease that afflicted you could bring one's own mortality to mind; she believed that Zach feared diabetes would be the cause of an ultimate loss in her life, be it himself or a child. But she knew there were no guarantees. Life was meant to be taken as it came, reveling in the happy times and accepting the ones that weren't so good.

"What are you doing out here?" Zach asked, closing the screen door quietly behind him. He walked over and propped his hip against the porch railing, shoving his tousled hair back before the hand slipped down to cover a yawn.

"Thinking."

"What have you decided?" There was an unusual tenseness in his voice.

"I wasn't making a decision. You're not on trial, Zach."

"I didn't mean. . ."

"Sure you did. Tell me the truth. Do you feel I'm working this situation overtime?"

He shrugged, his enigmatic expression saying little. "I want you to have your answers."

"Stop patronizing me," Casey insisted. "You were always a man with an opinion. Usually not the same as mine."

"I want you to be happy."

"Then be yourself. If you're sick of the situation, say so."

He spread his hands regretfully and shrugged again, "Okay. I'd love for you to understand my psychoses. I'd love to understand them myself, but I don't. I probably could ask myself why a billion times a day and admit there are no more answers than those I gave you. I'm sorry. I don't want to take chances with our children."

"Thank you. I appreciate your honesty. And I can't help but feel your 'don't know' could last a lifetime."

Even in the dark, his unrelenting scrutiny was unnerving. "You want a time frame? A child in three months? Six months? A year?"

"Not if you won't give me one."

"I can't, but I need to know what our future holds too."

"Right now, it's working out this problem that's eating away at our marriage," Casey said. "I'm not testing you to see if you give the perfect answer. I am trying to see my. . .our lives without children. To tell you the truth, I'm having problems, but I don't blame you. It wouldn't be any different if I'd been the reason, and we were dealing with that. When I think about not becoming a mother, I have this feeling, almost like bereavement."

Zach turned to stare out over the lake. "No woman should be deprived of something she wants so badly, Casey." The words were very emotional.

"It's not that simple," she said, her foot scraping the floor as she drew the swing to a halt. "I want it all. What's a child when the father isn't the man you love? And that would be the case since I'm not likely to stop loving you."

"And so it all comes down to choices. If we can't have children, do we accept the fact and try to make each other happy? Or does the pain destroy our marriage?"

"I don't know, Zach. I just don't know."

nine

Casey came out of the bedroom, dressed in shorts and a T-shirt. "Wish I didn't have to drive into Wilmington for this appointment. I should have rescheduled. Sure you won't come with me?"

Zach shook his head and tried to stand. The grimace of pain as he fell backward on the sofa shocked Casey into movement.

"What's wrong?"

"My leg's cramping. So bad I can hardly stand."

"We need to get you to the doctor."

Zach shook his head. "There's nothing he can do. I'll take the muscle relaxers and lie down. By the time you get home, it'll be over."

"How do you know?" Casey demanded, certain he was keeping secrets.

"Actually, I don't. I have no idea what's causing the cramps, but I talked to David a few minutes ago. He seemed to think it's to be expected. Told me to take my medication and stay off my leg for a day or so. If I'm not better by early next week, I'll go in for an exam."

"Let me call and cancel the appointment."

Zach grabbed Casey's hand as she walked past. "No. I'll be fine, probably asleep before you're out of the driveway. Those pills knock me out."

"You shouldn't be here alone."

"Casey, I'm a big boy. Go."

She hesitated a few moments longer, torn over leaving him to fend for himself. Finally, she asked, "You staying on the couch or getting back in bed?"

"Might as well go to bed. Where are my crutches?"

She retrieved them from the corner where they'd leaned for the past several days. "I thought we were through with these things."

"We are," Zach insisted. "Just a little setback. You'll see. I'll be fine by the time we go home next week."

Casey retrieved the cordless phone from the living room and returned it to the cradle. "Here's the phone. Are you sure?"

"Go. I've got your cellular number. I'll call if I can't live without one of your bran shakes," he teased.

"Maybe I should mix a pitcher before I go and leave them on the nightstand."

Zach stretched and yawned widely. "No, thanks. Too sleepy to wait."

Casey chuckled and kissed him good-bye. "Try that line again *after* you take your pills."

ð

As she drove down the dirt road, Casey couldn't help but worry about Zach and his relapse. What had caused the muscle cramps? She should make a call of her own.

Last night's conversation played around in her head. Casey considered the revelations to be a double-edged sword. She was confused, and no doubt Zach felt the same. The tenseness remained after they went to bed, neither sleeping as they considered the options. Admittedly, only time could provide the answers they sought so desperately. Yet time seemed their biggest adversary. Could she wait days, months, maybe years to become a mother?

Finally, in the dark hours of early morning, they discussed the possibilities. A genetic counselor was first on her list. She planned to ask her doctor for a referral today. If her prayers were answered, she would convince Zach to make an informed decision as to whether they could have a child of their own or adopt.

"Dear Lord," she whispered softly, "You give so much, and yet all I do is ask for more. Please lift the pain from Zach's body and restore him to the man he was before this all happened. Bring him back to You. And Lord, if it's Your will that we have a child, please open his heart and make him receptive to what You would have for us. Help Zach understand he cannot do this alone, and help our marriage to withstand this difficult time."

As always, the sweet peace of entrusting her concerns to her Heavenly Father stole over Casey. She tuned the radio to the gospel station and sang along.

❧

Steven Meares had been her personal physician for as long as Casey could remember. Their relationship went further than doctor/patient or colleagues. They were friends. After their greeting, Casey asked after Elizabeth, his wife.

"Doing great. Marking off the days until the baby comes."

Casey swallowed the knot in her throat at the thought. "Tell her to hang in there. Won't be long now."

Steven nodded. "How's Zach?"

She latched onto the question like a lifeline, forcing the envy from her thoughts. "He'd actually been doing better until he woke with leg cramps this morning. He talked to David Burns, and he's not concerned."

"We're so glad he's back on his feet. Elizabeth ran into Stacey the other day, and she said he seems good as new."

"I don't think there will be any long-term problems."

"Let's get this examination over with and then we can talk."

Steven asked a few general questions and shocked her by deciding to run a test to totally rule out the possibility of pregnancy.

"Get dressed and come to my office."

Casey slipped into her clothes and moved across the hall. Impatient to be on her way home, she waited several long, tense minutes before he joined her.

"Okay, what's up?" he asked, settling into the chair next to hers. "I thought you two were ready to start a family."

She grimaced. "That's something I need to discuss with you. We need the name of a good genetic counselor."

The story came slowly at first, and then picked up as Casey voiced her concerns and fears. "I don't know why he's reacting like this."

"Who can figure the human psyche?" Steven asked. "This could pass as quickly as it came."

"I don't know," Casey said doubtfully. "I've never seen him like this. Zach doesn't even want to think about a baby. He gets upset when I try to pin him down timewise, but what if this problem never goes away?"

"That's a question only you can answer."

Casey knew that to be true. "He's terrified I could conceive accidentally. I need a prescription so I can relieve him of that one worry."

"I'll write the prescription, but let's get the test results back before you get it filled."

Casey stared at him, afraid to ask the question in her head. "You can't possibly think. . .?"

"I need to rule out every possibility," he offered. "What if I do some checking and call you with a referral?"

"That'll work. Zach and I will be at Solitude through Saturday. We'll be back in town next week."

Steven reached for a prescription pad and scratched the information for the pharmacy.

"Let's get together soon. I know Elizabeth is eager to see you both."

❧

After her visit, Casey chatted with the nurses for a few minutes and then felt drawn to call their pastor to see if he had to see her.

Thankful to find the church office fairly quiet for a change, she spoke to the secretary and followed her instructions to go right in.

"Casey," Franklin said, standing and coming around the desk to hug her. "How are you? I can't tell you how we've missed having you in church."

"I've missed being here. Stomped on any toes lately?"

He shrugged and grinned. "With a congregation the size of ours, it's hard not to touch on a topic that doesn't impact someone."

Grace Fellowship had been her church home all her life. As a child, she had spent time in the nursery, Sunday school, vacation Bible school, youth church, and then young singles activities. When she and Zach started dating, he joined the church, and after their wedding, they naturally joined the newly married Sunday school class. It was a fun group, and they were always planning some activity. She particularly enjoyed the Bible study classes where they rotated from home to home.

A new addition, Pastor Franklin Benton had come to their church shortly after the minister who married them was called to the missionary fields.

"How's Zach?"

Once she started talking, Casey found it was like a dam bursting open. "I'm afraid, Franklin. I just feel in my heart that he's not trusting in the Lord right now."

"He's had quite an experience."

"If that were all, I could accept it was the accident. But he's looking at our lives through a medical perspective, not at what

God wants or expects of us, but fearful of what the doctor in him says can happen."

"Would it help if I visited?"

"Maybe. We'll be back in town by the weekend. If his leg's better, we'll attend church Sunday."

"Be patient, Casey. I know it's difficult, but God will show you the way. He'll show Zach too."

"I hope so. I'm so confused right now. Feeling elated we're together again and despairing that we'll ever get back to the way we were."

He raised his brows. "Have you considered God doesn't want you to return to that place? People grow out of trials and tribulations. Could be God's showing you the new place He wants for you both."

"Do you think God doesn't have a place in our lives for children?"

"I couldn't say. Maybe now isn't the time to bring a little one into the world."

"Maybe not. Did I tell you Zach plans to go into pediatric research?"

"What will that entail?"

"I have no idea. I don't know if it's something he can do here or if we'll end up at a teaching hospital or research center."

"Does that bother you?"

"Not half as much as being without Zach. I love him. I've been very angry because he made decisions that affected us both, but I still love him with all my heart. I wish I could make him understand that sickness and health were more than words in the ceremony."

He smiled broadly. "There's a Scripture. Let me find it for you."

Casey watched as he thumbed through his well-worn leather Bible. "Here it is. First Corinthians 7:4, 'The wife hath not power of her own body, but the husband: and likewise also the husband hath not power of his own body, but the wife.' When you spoke your vows, you became one. Then this happened, and Zach forgot to keep his eyes on God. But he did it to protect you."

The words sank into her mind. Zach made the wrong decision for the right reason. "Pray for us, please."

"We do, Casey. You and Zach have been on our heart and we know God is working great things in your lives."

"Thank you for seeing me, Franklin. Give Emily my love."

"I look forward to seeing you back in the congregation soon. Let's pray together before you go."

❧

Lunchtime had passed by the time she headed home to Zach. She made one last visit before leaving the city, stopping by David's office. The orthopedic doctor confirmed what Zach told her that morning and suggested she see to it that he took it easy for a couple of days.

"I can do that. I worry that he keeps things from me."

"Not this time. This is a temporary setback."

"You sound like Zach."

"You've done an excellent job, Casey. Given the extent of his injuries, I expected Zach to be down much longer. I fully attribute his remarkable recovery to your presence."

"Don't give the credit to me. Many a prayer has been offered up for Zach's recovery."

"Yes. Including a few of my own."

Casey's eyes fixed on David. "David, has Zach ever said anything to you about the problems he's having?"

"You mean his leg?"

She shook her head, wondering if she should continue. "No. Zach is obsessed with the idea that he could pass on his diabetes to any children we might have."

"When did this come about?"

"It's the reason he left." She sighed heavily. "I wish I understood this fear that's driving him. Sorry, didn't mean to dump our troubles on you."

"Don't be silly. Our goal is to get Zach back to normal, mentally as well as physically. Now, how can I help?"

❧

Calling home, she found him awake and hungry. Casey promised a surprise and stopped at the little place next to the grocery store. Zach insisted they had the best hamburgers in the county, and though she agreed, a burger was not what she wanted. She ran into the grocery store for a pint of her favorite ice cream.

At home she found Zach had made his way to the sofa. "I thought you were going to stay off that leg."

"I used my crutches."

Casey set her bags on the countertop. "Still hungry? I got you a burger and fries."

"Bring them on."

Zach sat up, resting his leg on a pillow on the wide coffee table. She carried the tray over to him, feeling almost guilty when she removed the ice cream and spoon.

"I can eat this later if you prefer."

"Please don't deprive yourself of the things you want on my account," Zach insisted.

The words lingered heavily on the air as both recognized the far-reaching impact of his words.

How did he fight the temptations? Casey could easily recall the times they ate in restaurants or dined at the homes of friends. Their best friends knew he was a diabetic and planned the menu accordingly. Zach always refused desserts. In fact, he'd eaten only a bite of wedding cake for their picture.

Refusing must be doubly hard for children, having to say

no to the things children craved. Just say no. For diabetic children, that meant saying no to anything that could send them into a coma. Zach was right. It wasn't fair they should be dealt such a rotten hand. Maybe she could help with this research project. The disease touched her life too.

She'd changed her eating habits when they married. Occasionally she had a craving for something like ice cream, but Casey rarely brought sweets into their house.

"I went by to see Franklin," Casey offered. "He said they miss us."

Zach continued eating. "So, did you tell him about us? About me?" he asked, feigning nonchalance.

Casey shrugged. "Well. . .yes. He's praying for us."

"What makes you so sure that will help?" Zach countered.

Shocked speechless, Casey stared at him. "Are you blaming our problems on God?" she asked finally.

"Why, Casey? Why us? We're good people. We attend church faithfully, tithe, study His word, and serve in every way possible. Why can't things be like they were?"

"Franklin says God's using this experience to help us grow."

"By making us suffer?"

"Would you turn to Him if life never had any bumps? Have you turned to Him since this happened?" His feigned interest in his food didn't cover his lack of response. "God's given us so much, Zach. David says you've made remarkable progress."

"David? What did you do, Casey?" he demanded. "Check up on me? Don't you trust me to tell you the truth?"

"I wanted to be sure there was nothing I could do to help."

"Who else did you check in with?" he asked, shoving the tray onto the coffee table.

"You're being ridiculous. I wasn't checking up on you."

A storm brewed in his blue eyes. "Sure seems like it to me."

"I can't talk to you when you're like this." Casey stared

into her ice cream carton.

The silence stretched for several minutes as each sat, wondering what had happened.

"I'm sorry." Zach was the first to offer an apology. "I know you were looking out for my best interests."

"I'm sorry too. I did check up on you. Maybe it's a built-in defense mechanism. You've always been so protective. I was afraid you weren't telling me something."

"And you're feeling cautious, afraid I'll hurt you again?"

"We do have the power to hurt those we love more than others."

Zach withdrew, his eyelids lowering. "I blame myself for making you have doubts."

Casey shook her head. "I blame myself for not seeing what was going on. I should have known you were unhappy."

"I wasn't. I was very happy. And then in one moment it hit me that I could destroy our happiness and you with the truth. Until then, I actually believed I could father a child, and we would never have any dark clouds hovering over our heads. But there's always a dark cloud, ready to rain on my parade."

"Not always," Casey whispered. "There's good along with the bad."

"Casey, I was born when Mom was twenty-five. I grew up between Wilmington and here, a much-loved, overindulged child. Graduated, went off to college, and then I got sick. When my diabetes was diagnosed, we went through it all, especially the anxiety and guilt. After it was under control, I went back to school.

"Mom called at least five times a day. She wanted me to come home, and I used my illness to manipulate her. That was tough on her because as you know my mother likes to be in control."

"As does her son," Casey pointed out.

"As does her son," he agreed.

"Actually, she blamed herself for my disease. Dad called to say she was taking it pretty badly. I think that's the reason he wanted to sell everything and travel. He thought she'd mothered one child too long."

"Did it stop?"

"We came to terms. Mom realized she had to let me handle my life and accept that she wasn't at fault."

"But she didn't let go completely." That explained a lot to Casey. Zach's beliefs that his disease caused his mother grief and anxiety affected their marriage as well.

"I know I keep harping on that day," Zach said, "but when I think of that child's mother, I see your face in my mind and hear Mom blaming herself. I had to protect you."

"Oh, my love, who's going to protect you?" Casey asked, moving to hug him tightly.

Zach was silent. Their separation had been a traumatic experience for him. If only she'd known what he was feeling. But she couldn't have. He couldn't blame himself either. Together, they had to find an answer to their dilemma.

The tempest calmed and they ate in companionable silence.

Minutes later, Casey licked the spoon and dropped it into the ice cream carton. "I'm stuffed."

Zach looked as though he were weighing a question. "I've never known you to eat like that before. I kept expecting you to explode."

"Funny. Maybe I'm just very happy."

"If ice cream makes you happy, I'll buy a few gallons."

He reached for his glass of diet soda on the coffee table and took a sip. "Sweet tooth satisfied?" She nodded and he asked, "Can I have my dessert now?"

Casey eyed him suspiciously. What was he talking about? Surely he wasn't going to demand ice cream or candy.

"You're my sweet," he said matter-of-factly. "I'm surprised these lips don't put me right into a coma."

"Then maybe you shouldn't. . . ," Casey began, laughing delightedly as his lips brushed hers.

ॐ

Zach spent the next day in bed, insisting the cramps weren't as bad, but Casey knew he was hurting. When he tried to make plans for the day, she insisted he take his medication and rest. He slept through lunch, and she prepared an early dinner.

She started to lift the tray, stopping to answer the phone.

"Casey, glad I caught you."

"Steven?" she asked.

"I've been tied up at the hospital all day. Three new mothers decided today was the day. I've been running around like crazy. You didn't fill that prescription, did you?"

The first vestiges of fear began to stir within her. "I was waiting to hear from you."

"Good. You're not going to need them."

Her heart plummeted as Steven shared his news. She stifled the urge to ask if he was certain. How was she going to tell Zach? "But how?"

"You took antibiotics when you had the flu. Not to mention you could be in the small percentile where birth control fails. By the way, I made an appointment with the genetics counselor. It's imperative that we jump right on that."

"Oh, Steven, this is not good news. Not now."

"It's wonderful news, Casey. Everything will work out. You just wait and see."

She glanced up when Zach walked into the room carrying his crutches.

"Okay, thanks for calling," she said, hurriedly replacing the receiver and directing her next question at Zach. "Shouldn't those be under your arms?"

"The pain's gone. Just as quickly as it came." He dropped onto the sofa and lifted his leg. "Who was that?"

"Steven," she said automatically. The pastor's words rolled into her head. *Not her body.*

"What did he want?"

"Referral on a genetics counselor. I asked while I was there." It wasn't a total lie. The appointment had been made. Pregnancy was no longer a remote possibility—it was reality and the expediency of the situation had become immediate.

"Good idea. Are you feeling okay?" Zach asked. "You're looking a little pale."

"I'm fine," she mumbled, turning to lift his tray. *Tell him,* the little voice in her head shouted, but Casey pushed it back. "Do you want soda or water with your dinner?"

"Ice water would taste wonderful."

Casey delivered his meal and brought her plate over to the armchair. She ate in numbed silence. How could this be? She had made Zach a promise. He would feel so betrayed. *It wasn't intentional,* she defended silently.

"Earth to Casey. Did you hear me?"

She shook her head and glanced at him. "Sorry."

"I asked if you're ready to go home tomorrow."

"Are you up to the trip?" At his nod, she added, "There's a lot to be done. I have to pack and straighten up around here. What time did Stacey say she was leaving for the airport?"

"Hey, slow down. We'll get there with time to spare. This chicken is great. Why aren't you eating?"

"I'm not hungry." That was no lie. Steven's news had taken her appetite. "I think I'll start packing."

Casey returned her plate to the kitchen and disappeared into the bedroom. The cheval mirror caught her eye as she walked by and she stopped to take a look. There was little change in her appearance beyond a small weight gain. How could it be? She was certain the test read negative. What was she going to do?

Tears welled and ran down her cheeks as she considered how Zach would react to this news. Just as suddenly, a burst of anger shot through her. Her happy news was being negated by worry. It wasn't fair.

"Casey?"

She hurriedly wiped her eyes and pulled out a dresser drawer. "What did you want to wear home tomorrow?"

"Shorts and a T-shirt are fine. You want some help?"

"You shouldn't be on that leg. Those cramps might return."

"I'm wearing the brace."

"Just relax. I'll take care of this."

Zach wandered back into the family room, his thoughts on Casey's strange behavior. Was she coming down with something? The doctor in him knew "no appetite" and "pale as a ghost" weren't normal.

He started to ask and then realized she would have told him if she weren't feeling well. That was one thing about his wife. She didn't keep secrets from him.

ten

Hours later Casey repressed the sigh that rose to her throat as she looked out over the lake. There had never been a more idyllic place. Maybe because she and Zach spent only happy times here. He'd known exactly where to win her back.

"Do we have to go?" she asked as he pulled the last box from the porch.

"Stacey's waiting."

"She gets her vacation, and we get the guest house." Casey turned to Zach. "We could go back to our house. I could run over to Mom and Dad's every day."

"I sold the house," Zach said.

"Sold? When?"

"Last week."

"It wasn't on the market," Casey objected. "Another secret?" Realization hit her almost immediately. That was certainly sanctimonious. The sale of the house was nothing compared to the secret she was keeping.

"I listed it when I first came back," Zach admitted, a new grimness in his expression. "I spoke with the agent when we went to the grocery store last week. The buyer wants to move in right away."

"Would it have been too much for you to ask my opinion on the matter?" Casey turned away from him.

Zach slid the box into the back of the truck and stepped forward. "Another stupid act," he said tersely. "I'd think by now you'd expect me to act like an idiot."

She had no intention of falling prey to his self-directed

scorn. "Actually, I prefer you behaving as one half of this couple. Discounting the fact that it was your house, and you had every right to put it on the market without my approval. . ."

"Something else we never got around to correcting," Zach said quickly. "There's no excuse for what I did. Other than the fact that I wanted to surprise you."

"You did that."

"I was tying up loose ends. Working on capital for the new house."

"You already have the agent looking, don't you?"

His guilty expression confirmed Casey's suspicions, just as her own face mirrored her despair.

"This one will have your approval," Zach promised.

"Our house had my approval. I'll miss it."

"Not too much I hope. I mean," he paused and then rushed on, "it never really suited your antiques."

"Antiques fit anywhere. Why the sudden change of heart, Zach? Once upon a time I couldn't have paid you to live in—what was it you called them? Oh yeah, drafty old mausoleums."

"I realized the only one who did any real giving in our marriage was you."

"Oh, that's not true," Casey objected sarcastically. "You were always giving me things."

"Apparently not the things that counted. You'd have been so much happier in the house you wanted."

"I was happy in our house. With you."

"I want to give you the things you deserve. If we can't have a child. . ."

Tell him, the little niggling voice said. She had to. But how? What could she say to make him understand the situation was in God's hands now? "I neither want nor expect you to compensate me for the lack of anything in our lives, Zach."

"You make me feel like a jerk."

Casey flung her hands out in simple annoyance. "I don't mean to. I want you to realize I'm there for you, whether it's selling the house or dealing with your disease. I see how diabetes affects you and understand it's a valid concern for you. I also know I can't fully understand. But I can't pretend to like this protective tendency of yours. I'm involved in this relationship too. I'll never be happy allowing you to make all the decisions. I'm not the type."

"I'm sorry, Casey."

"I believe you are, but you're going to have to stop apologizing and start thinking." She lifted the last of a loaf of bread from the box. "Let's feed this to the ducks."

The midmorning sun was already very warm, its brilliant light glinting silver on the smooth surface of the still water. Casey felt transfused with tranquility as she took a deep breath and released it slowly.

"I've grown so fond of them," she said, tossing the crumbs to the ducks that floated just inches away from their feet. "Let's get a duck pond and take them home with us."

Zach slipped an arm about her waist and said, "They'd waddle down to the river and hop the first ship to heaven-only-knows-where and you'd never even get a postcard."

Casey sighed. "Then I'll have to visit them here. You might as well get ready, Zachary Taylor. We're going to keep the road hot."

"Just the two of us. Here. Hmmm," he purred with satisfaction. "My idea of paradise." His lips descended slowly toward hers.

A paradise named Solitude. Did it mean their life would only be happy when they were alone together? Casey hoped not. She wanted to be closer to Zach, but she also needed others to complete her world. Just as she needed the baby growing within her—their gift from God.

"You and me, anywhere, is my idea of paradise," Casey said, leaving his arms.

"Hey, where are you going?" he called out in surprise when she started toward the house.

"Home. You coming?"

❧

Stacey dragged the heavy bag out into the hallway and fixed a soulful, pleading gaze on Zach.

"Okay, I'll get the rest of them."

Casey lowered the letter she was reading and glanced up when Stacey came to stand before her, an inquiring look on her face.

"Well?"

"What?" Casey asked with raised brows, uncertain what her sister wanted.

"Are you happy?" Exasperation tinged the question.

"Yes. Very. We've done some serious talking. For the first time, I have a good perspective on how he feels."

"Does he know how you feel?"

Casey stood and hugged her twin. "He knows what I expect. Thanks for caring, Stacey."

"You're welcome, sis."

Zach came out of Stacey's room, loaded with two bags and an overnight case. "Are you leaving for vacation or forever?" he demanded, scrambling to catch the bag that slipped from under his arm. "What are you two plotting now?" he added as the women shared a smile.

"Nothing," Stacey said with questionable innocence.

"Oh, my knee."

The sudden groan as he dropped the suitcases brought Casey to his side immediately. "Zach?" she cried in alarm, grasping his arm. "Did you hurt—"

"You promised to protect me from her," he whispered.

Casey chuckled with the happy memory. "Drive her to the airport, Zach," she instructed, loud enough for Stacey to hear. She helped him gather the bags and turned to Stacey, hugging her sister close. "Have a nice vacation."

"I probably won't have as much fun as you and Prince Charming here." When Casey started to protest, Stacey squeezed her hand, "Don't worry, Case. He lives for my teasing. Right, Zach?"

He grinned broadly. "Yes, evil twin, I do."

Casey laughed at their antics.

"Take care," Stacey said, hugging Casey one last time.

"You, too. Don't have too much fun in Hawaii."

"I'll try not to. By the way, your favorite group is singing at church tonight."

Casey shut the door behind her husband and sister and wondered what she should do with the first time she'd spent alone in weeks. Unpack? Call the hospital? Check the house?

She didn't want to do the first. And she'd wait until Zach came back to go to the house. That left the hospital. Time to call the Nursing Director. Let her know she was back, ready to return to work and resume a normal life. Maybe that could wait another week. Just until they settled in—after she shared the news about the baby with Zach. Another week wouldn't make that much of a difference.

❧

"How about dinner out tonight? We could attend the evening service."

"Are you. . ." Casey stopped herself. She wasn't going to question his motives. Sooner or later she'd learn exactly what was going on. "Sounds great. Any special place?"

The grandfather clock bonged the hour. "We'll need to find something fast if we want to get to church on time," Casey said.

They locked up and Zach drove to a burger place.

He unloaded their tray onto a table. "I still say we should invest in one of these places. The return is probably better than my percentage of the practice."

"I can see your stationery now," Casey said, using her hand to demonstrate the layout in the air. "Zachary Taylor, M.D., and right under that—Franchise Owner."

"I bet Mom never discouraged Dad."

"Maybe not, but there are already investment opportunities galore in our family. Save your money, sweetie. One day soon I'm going to need it for Bordeaux-Taylor Enterprises."

"Just think how much more you'd have if I invested it now."

"Maybe I should give it more thought." Casey dabbed at her mouth. "Stacey's flight get off on time?"

"She barely made it. Had the time twisted. Thought the departure time was 5:50 and it was 5:05. How she runs the advertising department is beyond me."

"Actually she's quite ingenious. Stacey hates to fly. I think those little memory lapses are her way of giving herself less time to think. She always manages not to miss her plane."

"You understand her pretty well, don't you?"

"The flip side of my personality. Any trait I lack can usually be found in my sister."

"At least she's out of our hair," he said with a nod of his head.

"Two weeks isn't all that long, you know."

"Don't remind me. I'd better call that agent tomorrow. Rush her up."

Casey eyed him for a moment. "We're not taking the first place she shows us."

"Would I do that?"

"The first chance you got."

"I'm just a bystander in this deal," he argued, seasoning his baked potato. "You're picking this house."

"No, I'm not," Casey said. "We're joined at the hip in this venture." She glanced at her watch. "We're going to be late."

ಜ

The music was all she remembered. Casey felt revived by the group's songs of worship. They waited in line to offer their thanks and then moved toward the exit. Franklin greeted members and guests alike, inviting them to return for services the following week.

"Casey," he called joyously. "It's so wonderful to have you back."

"Thank you. The music was so uplifting. Exactly what I needed tonight."

"You sound a bit down."

She glanced over to where Zach stood chatting with a deacon. "We're going to need your prayers again."

"Things haven't improved? Zach appears to be doing fine."

"I received some surprising news this week and don't know how to tell him."

"God is always helpful during times of trouble."

"I know," came her soft aside as Zach joined them. She smiled and slipped her hand into his.

"Good to have you back in the house of the Lord, Zach."

Casey was surprised by his lack of response.

"We'd better get home, Casey. You wanted to check out your parents' house. Good night, Franklin."

"Good night."

Zach unlocked the car door and held it wide for her. Casey climbed inside and waited until he joined her. "That wasn't very polite of you."

"What did I do?" he asked, sounding just a touch too innocent.

She sighed. "Let's go home, Zach."

The trip was quiet, neither of them talking.

From the guest house driveway, Casey took the path toward her parents' home. Zach followed. She flicked the flashlight's beam toward the mansion's windows and doors. At the front door, she punched in the security code.

He followed her inside, pointing out a Victorian shelf clock. "That's new."

"Yes. Incredible, isn't it?"

"It's different," Zach said.

Casey laughed, the sound echoing through the house. The piece was too large and ornate for his tastes. He liked clean, simple lines. "You can't fool me. You don't like it."

"Well, no, but there are several pieces I do like."

"Maybe we can talk Mom and Dad into selling us a few of these. Stacey certainly doesn't want any antiques."

"Can we talk about earlier?" he asked suddenly.

"Sure. Let me check the house and we'll go home."

Running through her parents' home was impossible, Zach realized, as Casey's attention caught on various things. She made notes for the cleaning crew and stopped to admire other new additions placed here and there throughout the rooms.

"I've counted ten new pieces here in the house," she told Zach as he came into the drawing room.

"I thought you told me a dealer couldn't be a collector."

"Sell what you buy," Casey said with a nod of her head. "Don't be fooled into believing they wouldn't part with any of this. I know for a fact that the moment a profit was offered, almost anything would be sold."

"Almost?"

"There are some real treasures here. True finds they'll never sell. Family heirlooms meant to be passed on for generations. Let's go."

"Finished looking?"

"You're tired. I can come back another time."

Zach led the way through the shrubs that separated the guest house from the main house. He unlocked the door and moved through the rooms, turning on lights.

Casey followed, flipping switches and dimming lamps. "If you plan to live on a research grant, you'll have to learn frugality." She pulled the pot from the coffeemaker. "Decaf?"

"We'd better if we plan to get any sleep tonight."

"I'll probably be awake anyway," Casey said. She couldn't put off telling him much longer. Already she was a basket case. She walked to the living room and settled on the sofa, watching Zach over the rim of her cup as she sipped and settled it back into the saucer with a determined clatter. "Why were you rude to Franklin tonight?"

Zach set his mug on the end table and frowned. He rose and located a coaster, hurriedly sliding it under the cup's bottom. "I didn't mean to be. I just got that 'old rut' feeling."

"Why are you afraid?" Casey pushed her cup and saucer onto the table.

"I don't know."

"The rut never existed. We were busy but we always had time for each other. You can't freeze time, Zach."

"I wish."

"I don't. We have to see if our marriage is strong enough to forge ahead. This afternoon I actually considered putting off calling the hospital because of the same doubts. I'm calling tomorrow. It's time you checked in with your practice. You need to share your plans with Donald."

"I'll never make it out of the office without seeing patients."

"You could work half-days until you finish the grant request."

"I want to start the research now."

"Even if you don't get the grant?"

"Maybe I could work part-time to help generate enough

cash to keep us going," he suggested.

"There's enough in the bank to finance at least a year. Enough to support us too. Our parents would supplement if you needed longer."

"I want to do this myself."

"Alone?"

"You know what I mean."

Casey pleated the fabric of her skirt, smoothing it with shaking hands. *Lord, help me,* she cried inwardly. "I understand the accomplishment factor, but you should be willing to accept others' help in this venture. Where the money comes from doesn't matter as long as the end result is positive."

"True."

"Then we're in agreement," Casey said. "We get on with our respective lives, including work. We see our friends and family. And we remember we love each other."

Zach extended his coffee cup toward her. "It's unanimous."

eleven

Casey glanced at her watch and laid the book she'd been reading on the table. Time to rouse Zach from those stacks of papers and books he'd become so engrossed in.

Things were going pretty much to plan—his plan. She'd let Zach talk her into putting off calling the hospital.

"You planned to do your research on genetic counseling," he said when she hesitated over her final decision. "Why can't we do that first? We did say three months."

This reasoning had been difficult to reject, and then Ben had a bout of flu and she'd spent a couple of days helping out at the store. Of course, selling antiques was more pleasure than burden, and this change of plans gave her no anxiety pangs.

Next, Zach scheduled a visit to the real estate agent's office. "I'll defer to your judgment on this one. You're the expert at these places."

"These places?" she repeated. "It's going to be your home, Zach. You need to be comfortable."

"And I will be. As long as you're there when she starts asking what we're looking for."

The agent's reminder to remove their furnishings from the house required more complicated planning as they attempted to find storage. Several special pieces of furniture, dishes, and collectibles couldn't be stored just anywhere. Casey spent hours rearranging the store's stockroom for them.

"What if they sell something?" Zach asked.

"It's marked. I feel better knowing it's there with an alarm than in storage."

And then Zach talked her into going with him to meet with his partner. Donald had been very understanding, and agreed to bring in a third doctor for the year. After that, they would look at the situation once Zach decided whether to continue his research or return to the practice.

Funny thing was, there hadn't been much discussion involved. All Zach had to do was mention doing something together, and she was ready, willing, and able. *Just a little while longer,* Casey kept promising herself.

She strolled into the kitchen and announced, "Time for dinner."

"Where's your list?" he asked over his shoulder.

"On the pink legal pad."

"Pink?" he teased.

"Too feminine for you?"

Zach worked his arm, his muscles bulging underneath the short sleeve of the polo shirt. "Give me a man's color."

Casey brushed her fingers through his tousled hair and leaned against his shoulder while he studied the paper.

"When is that appointment with the genetic counselor?"

"What appointment?" she asked. Guiltily, Casey turned her attention to stacking papers in neat piles.

"The one Steven made for you."

"Oh, that," Casey said, picking up a pen and scribbling on her legal pad. "I need to ask."

"I thought you said he'd already made one," Zach said.

"He did," she exclaimed, the bottom dropping from her stomach. "I forgot to write it down. I'll call tomorrow."

❧

"Good, you're home," Zach said, grabbing his keys from the table. "The agent called and wants us to go look at a house. She said she's found what we're looking for. We'll have to hurry. I have an interview with the grants committee at three."

At her lack of response, Zach demanded, "Casey? Did you hear me? She thinks she's found your house."

"Our house," Casey corrected automatically. "Zach, we need to talk."

"What's wrong?"

"Nothing as far as I'm concerned, but you might feel differently."

His expression stilled and grew serious. "Casey?"

"I saw my doctor this morning."

"Did you get the appointment information?"

"I'm pregnant," Casey blurted. "Ten weeks."

"You can't. . . You can't have this baby."

The fierce sparkling in his eyes shocked her. "This child is a miracle, Zach." Casey spoke with deliberate firmness. She had to make him understand. "He or she was conceived that last morning before you left."

"You said we had time."

"I thought we did."

"And maybe you knew what you were doing all along." The angry retort hardened his features, the accusation hanging in the air between them. "Maybe that's why you decided you'd be generous and take hubby back. Well, you know how I feel." Zach turned away.

Casey felt ice spreading through her body, so cold she wondered if she'd ever feel warm again. "Yes, I know. I also know those accusations are part of the fear tearing you up inside. I think I understand your reasons for feeling that way, but I am going to have this child. I'll love and care for it, and make sure it's as happy and healthy as possible."

"I can't handle this."

"Then I won't ask you to. I know I said we'd wait, but I didn't know I was already pregnant. You can't hold me to something I said when I thought there was no hope."

"You never really understood how I feel."

"Probably not. I'm not even sure you understand, Zach. Life's too short to bog yourself down worrying about what could be. It was too late for you to save that child. It's too late to stop this pregnancy."

"You could abort the fetus. Then when we know more, when we're more certain, you could conceive again."

Casey closed her eyes and attempted to catch her breath, the horror of his words tearing at her. "This is not some John Doe fetus," she cried out. "This is our child." Zach turned his back on her and Casey came up behind him and slipped her arms about his waist. "Having a child is an extension of the vows we took on our wedding day, in sickness and in health. I won't stop loving you because you're a diabetic. And you won't stop loving me if I develop some sort of illness. I won't deny our child a chance to come into this world."

Zach shrugged himself from her hold. "I've got that interview. I don't know when I'll be back."

"Don't you mean *if*? Should I expect you in a month or so?" Casey demanded, her reasoning mode veering sharply to anger.

"I should have stayed away."

She clutched her trembling hands together and gave vent to the agony. "Where are you running to this time?"

"Don't push me, Casey."

"I made a promise to myself when I decided to give us a second chance. No regrets, Zach."

He stopped in midstride and turned to her. "You promised me time."

"Yes, I did—when I thought it was one of our choices," she repeated.

"It still is."

"Not for me. And not for you either if you're the man I thought you were. It wouldn't have mattered if you'd stayed away, Zach. God's will had already been done. What if your mother had made that decision?"

"You wouldn't have all this grief." His voice was rough with anxiety. "Just try to see my side of this."

"I have." Casey's resolve strengthened with the words. "I've struggled to understand exactly where this incredible fear came from, and I can't. I won't ask you to accept our child, Zach, but don't ask me to kill it."

Zach didn't look back as he stormed out the door. Casey refused to give vent to the tears. *He won't break my heart again,* she vowed as she rose and paced the room restlessly. She'd gone into this reconciliation knowing she could lose him again. Aware that it would hurt twice as much if she did.

But this time, Casey had something to prove. She would validate the fact that life could not be lived under a cloak of doom.

Casey went into the kitchen for a glass of cold water. She removed the empty pitcher from the refrigerator. Zach's doing. He never refilled the thing.

She turned the faucet on full force and cried out when she splattered herself. The container banged on the countertop. Why couldn't she get him out of her head? They had both been hurting when he left—her, because she'd been robbed of her excitement about their baby, and Zach, because of his fear.

Casey looked around the house for some task to take her mind off the situation. Everything was neat and in place, even Zach's research materials. How could there have been so much to do over the last few days and nothing when she needed something to occupy her now? The reason was simple. Everything had included Zach. Everything but the shop, that is.

The shop. Casey latched onto that thought and grabbed her purse. She'd spend a few hours in the one place she could depend on to restore normalcy to her off-base world.

Casey found losing herself in the past difficult when the present weighed so heavily on her mind. She chatted with a few browsers, turning them over to Ben when the facts refused to come to her head.

In the end, she went into the storeroom and looked over the new stock, her gaze drifting to their furniture. Her furniture thanks to Zach's generosity. Her treasures. Why couldn't he realize nothing was as important to her as him?

The hours passed, and the black of the moonless night suited her mood as Casey locked the door of the shop. She knew Ben was curious about her mood but was glad he hadn't asked any questions. Maybe he recognized the signs from the last experience. After he'd gone, she relived everything Zach had shared while they were at Solitude. Did he believe that not having children would guarantee them a life without problems?

If everything were normal, Zach would be home right now, telling her about his grant committee interview or discussing the house the realtor had shown them. Tears trailed down Casey's cheeks. She couldn't delay the inevitable. Her lonely, memory-filled home waited.

And as she feared, it was all there. The bedroom seemed filled with his scent, his possessions still scattered about. Zach had taken nothing, not even his briefcase.

Casey lifted it onto the bed and snapped the latches, staring down at the papers he'd spent hours preparing. How had he made the presentation? She closed it quickly. She couldn't bear to stay there another minute.

Like a caged animal, she considered her options. She'd go over to her parents' house. She wanted to look at the new things anyway. The beam of the flashlight bobbed up and down with the movement as it marked the trail. Casey cut through the shrubbery and went to the side door. Once inside she phoned the police department to report she was staying in the house. She didn't need a late night raid.

Her favorite chair was in the den, a colonial rocker her parents had bought before she and Stacey were born. Maybe they would loan it to her. *If only they were here now. Just to talk, to help me decide how to handle things. They would be so excited about the baby.* She could call them. No. She couldn't. She was an adult. This was her problem.

The creaking of the old rocker was a comforting sound.

The close look at how obsessed her husband was by his fear disturbed Casey. Why? Zach believed in God's miracles. She'd seen him pray at the bedside of a sick child. He often initiated or joined families in prayer. He believed in the validity of life.

The strident ring of the phone was unnerving. Casey took a couple of deep breaths as she reached out. Subconsciously, she hoped Zach would call when she'd forwarded the calls from the guest house.

"Casey? Is everything okay? I had this sudden feeling."

"Stacey," she cried, breaking into tears as disappointment overwhelmed her.

"What's wrong?"

"Zach's gone. I'm pregnant."

"I'm coming home."

Why did I blurt it out like that? "Stay in Hawaii, Stacey. Enjoy your vacation. There's nothing you can do here." Her protests sounded weak.

"Is it over for good?"

"I think so. Zach was floored by the news. I didn't mean for it to happen."

"Casey, you're not making sense. What are you saying?"

"I've never seen him this way. He's terrified. Haunted by these crazy fears that something will happen to the baby."

"I don't understand. What aren't you telling me?"

"He's afraid our child will inherit his diabetes and die."

"I'm coming home." This time Casey didn't argue. She needed Stacey. Her sister understood her in a way Zach never would. "I'll be there tomorrow. Take care of yourself."

Casey replaced the receiver and dropped her hands to her stomach. There was very little visible sign she was pregnant, just the slight bulge she'd attributed to eating after she'd regained her appetite.

She should have known but had been so wrapped up in her love for Zach that she had blocked out everything else. She swiped at the tears that trickled along the side of her jaw.

Their child would be a constant reminder of the past. And once Zach got beyond the terror that seemed to have taken root in his very soul, once he saw things weren't as hopeless as he thought, he'd be back. Until then, she needed a new plan.

She wouldn't go back to the hospital. Time for a clean break—no pitying looks or good-intentioned matchmakers. She could work at the shop and take the baby with her. Her parents would understand. There would be no question of her traveling, not when she had a child to raise.

She'd spend the rest of her life loving the child he'd given her. And that would be enough.

Overwhelming silence sharpened the loneliness she felt. Casey flipped on the radio. A contemporary Christian singer belted out the words "God is in control."

She couldn't stop herself from thinking things wouldn't be so bad if she and Zach had allowed God to control their lives. They called themselves Christians, but they had never given themselves to God completely. Even now, when she should be turning to Him for comfort, she was grieving like a mourning widow who had lost all hope of love.

A verse came to mind, and she went to the bookcase and

lifted the Bible from the shelf. Quickly thumbing through the
chapters, she stopped at Isaiah 54 and read His words of comfort directed at the widow, reassurances that even if the man
in her life had let her down, God would be her husband, her
giver of strength, the lover of her soul, the head of her house-
hold. Her child would never be fatherless because he would
have the greatest Father of all.

The Bible rested in her lap. "Heavenly Father, forgive my
failure to give You the proper place in my life. Forgive my
failure to give You my complete trust. I know You will see
me through this if only I ask and open my ears to listen when
I seek Your guidance. Thank You for loving me though I am
unworthy of the great gift You bestowed on me. Please rain
down Your blessings on Zach and this child growing in me."

twelve

Zach stopped walking and took a moment to realize where he was. In the early hours of the morning, no one strolled about the Riverfront Park that fronted the Cape Fear River, over-looking the USS *North Carolina* and the bridges entering the city. He didn't even remember the walk to the bench, just felt the cool, moist air wafting off the water.

He'd driven for hours, around and around, going no place in particular. And yet he couldn't drive away from her.

His semi-aware state was more like a nightmare unfolding in his subconscious. A nightmare where Casey moved farther and farther away. The last few days teased him, reminding Zach he couldn't live without her. She was too vital to his existence.

Without Casey's love he was no more than a shell of a man. His medicine, research—nothing was important without her.

Why now? Where was his chance to make Casey happy? His hope of getting himself past the fear that immobilized him?

Clenched fists struck his legs, bringing pain to the numb-ness that controlled his body. What was God trying to show him? Zach massaged his forehead. He believed in the healing powers of his Creator. He'd witnessed miracles in his line of work—healing that had more to do with God than medical science.

Casey was wrong to keep this from him, but in truth, he'd forced her hand—made her afraid of his reaction.

He loved children, so much so that he immediately decided

to dedicate his life to their well being. How could he have suggested she abort this baby? He didn't believe in abortion. That tiny fetus lived from conception, moving and growing long before the mother felt that first movement.

How could he expect Casey to base such a decision on "if"?

Nothing was certain. God brought them together for a reason.

The baby had been reality before he came back. If he hadn't returned, she would have had the child and provided it with a wealth of love.

Her miracle baby. Why couldn't he feel the same way about the child growing within his wife? Why couldn't he anticipate the joys of becoming a father, the hopes of seeing the child grow into a strong, healthy person of his or her own right?

Why couldn't he make things more right for the woman he loved? Why had he come back into her life? With all his promises and reassurances that he could make their life perfect. He'd always known it wasn't a perfect world. Just as he'd known he wasn't being fair to Casey. Why had this cursed idea buried its tentacles into his brain and refused to let go?

Zach rubbed at his eyes as tears boiled hotly. Men didn't cry. Hadn't his father told him that often enough? Even so, the thought didn't stop the tears.

Casey's love helped give his world meaning. Not his work. Just her love. He'd faced that when they were apart. Told himself he could convince her to see things his way. Deluded himself actually.

Had she lied to him about the test? She wasn't the sort to hide things. And she had been stunned by the news. He'd seen it in her eyes. The only difference was she saw a miracle, and all he could see was a life without her. Without her of his own choosing.

"Lord, show me the way," Zach cried out. "Give me an answer to this dilemma."

The phone booth in the distance seemed to beckon, to shout "Here's your answer." He moved quickly, fumbling as he pulled a phone card from his wallet and dialed. One ring. Two. Several before the connection. "Mom?"

"Zach? It's after two in the morning." Instantly, her voice changed, grew more awake, more concerned as she demanded, "Is something wrong? Where are you?"

Getting the words past the lump in his throat proved difficult. "Casey's pregnant."

"Darling, that's wonderful."

"I'm scared. Real scared."

"It's a natural reaction, honey," she soothed. "All first-time parents are."

"Are they afraid their child could die because it might inherit his father's diabetes?"

"Zach, where's Casey?"

He recognized the fear in his mother's voice. "I left her."

"Don't do this to her again, Zach. Go home. Confront the reality of the situation and deal with it. Your diabetes came as a shock. At first, it was an emotional nightmare. Your doctor kept telling me I had to calm down. Said my attitude could affect yours.

"It was difficult. I was so determined you would lead a normal life and yet I couldn't let go. I see that same tendency in you, in the way you treat Casey. You can't protect people from hurt, darling. You can comfort and soothe, but you can't play God and say what's going to happen in your life. Casey loves you. She married you knowing you had diabetes. She accepted that your children could have it too."

"She agreed to wait. To see a genetic counselor."

"How far along is she?"

"Ten weeks."

"Before you—"

"The day I left. I left to protect her and it was already too late."

"Why did you leave, Zach?"

"I lost a patient with diabetic complications."

"And?" she urged gently.

"His mother was devastated. I didn't want that to happen to Casey. I thought I could give her up, but I'm not strong enough."

"Strength has nothing to do with this. Your child was conceived in love. And love will bring you through."

"She'll never forgive me. I asked her to abort the baby."

"I think Casey's heart is big enough to forgive you many times over. If you give her the chance."

Zach leaned against the booth, his legs weakening with the thought of how much he loved Casey. Silence stretched across the lines, apprehension lacing his next question. "Mom, would you do it again?"

"Yes. Absolutely. Diabetes was such a small penalty for the pleasure of having you as my son. I love you, Zachary. Just as you are. I wouldn't change a thing."

"I love you, too, Mom."

"There's someone who loves you more—Jesus. I know you believe in God, but I'm not seeing evidence of it in your faith. Pray, Zach, and go home, darling. Casey needs you. You need her. She can help you through this if you let her."

"What if I fail?"

"You'll succeed. With God on your side, you can't fail. And Zach. . ."

"Yes?" he prompted when she hesitated.

"I'm glad you called me."

"You're going to make a pretty good grandmother."

"And you're going to be a great father. Pray for God's guidance. He's all the help you need."

And he definitely needed help, Zach realized, climbing into his vehicle and sitting behind the wheel, immersed in his thoughts.

His walk with Jesus had begun as a child of ten. Protected, loved, and spoiled, the only real suffering he'd known was his diabetes, and not even that was as bad as the other things he saw in the course of his work. Most of the time, when he was at his lowest, God gave him a wake-up call and showed him someone with greater struggles.

Maybe the mother and child had been a sign to show him he needed to slow down. Was he really afraid for Casey? Or himself? He couldn't keep pushing his body without consequences.

His religious life had long since taken a backseat to his marriage and career. Instead of walking hand in hand with God in all aspects of his life, he called upon Him when it was convenient.

But God never expected him to be perfect. He recognized and loved him for the person he was. He could be a better Christian, just as he could be a better husband, son, friend, and doctor. And when he thought about it, Zach realized all those other areas would improve if he were a better Christian.

If he trusted in God, they could make their marriage work. If he put his faith in the Father above, he could be a better father to his child. And if something should happen to him or Casey or the baby, they would all be more blessed to have known the bounty of God's love.

Zach rested his head on the steering wheel and prayed.

❧

Casey pulled the sheet over her body and lay back in the bed of her youth. She felt strangely satisfied with the realizations she'd made that night. And though her heart was breaking, she knew she and their child would survive with God's help.

If only Zach had given her the opportunity to prove how strong she could be. If only he could see that her strength fed off his love. She felt unconquerable with him by her side and so afraid without him. If only she could make him understand. Nothing mattered when you loved. Nothing but being loved in return.

If only. . . If only. . . The words filled her head time and time again as Casey's eyes drifted shut, a vision of Zach filling her head as sad tears spilled down her face.

≥●

Zach pounded on the door, his finger all but pressing the doorbell through the wall. When there was no response, he began to call her name, the wail resounding in the early morning darkness.

Casey stirred at the sound of Zach calling her name. She listened. Nothing. *Just a dream.* She lay down, and heard him again. She shot back up.

Padding to the window, she looked outside, her eyes stopping on the SUV, the interior light challenging the predawn darkness. He was back. Zach was home. Casey grabbed her robe and sped down the stairs and out the front door. As she burst through the shrubs, she stopped, staring at the man who leaned against the porch railing. "Zach?"

"I'm sorry. Please forgive me," he begged, nothing disguising the pleas that came from his heart. "I'm scared. I don't want to lose you."

"Oh, darling," she whispered, taking him into her arms. "I'm scared too, but I love you and this child enough to bear whatever comes our way. God will help us through this."

"It's not fair to you."

"Just love me. Understand that this child has to be born." Terror edged her thoughts while she waited for his response.

"I was wrong to ask you to do otherwise. I'll do anything. I'll get past this fear tearing at my insides and be a good husband and father. You'll see. I promise."

"I'll be there," Casey declared. "Loving you every step of the way."

"I love you."

Neither of them paid any attention to the wail of the sirens in the distance.

The blue strobe light revolved relentlessly as the patrol car turned into the driveway and the officers moved in their quest to locate the intruder.

"Go around back," one officer instructed, stopping as he came across the lone bedroom slipper.

His gaze rested on the vehicle in the distance, its lights still on, and the couple who stood in front of the guest house. It took him only seconds to recognize Zachary and Casey Taylor and wonder if she knew someone was breaking into her parents' home.

He cleared his throat loudly. "Excuse me, Dr. and Mrs. Taylor. The alarm over at the house went off. Perhaps you should go inside while we search the area."

Casey looked at Zach and laughter seized her voice. "It's me, Officer. I'm your prowler," she managed. "I completely forgot the alarm."

"I see." There was stern disapproval in his voice. "Perhaps you'd like us to accompany you while you lock up?"

"I'd appreciate it very much," she agreed quickly, squeezing Zach's hand as the officer followed them into the house and Casey reset the alarm.

&

After the eventful time, Casey expected to find herself in

exhausted slumber. Instead she lay studying Zach's face in the light of day. After hours of talking, he was finally asleep.

Casey thought about the fear that had a stranglehold on him and wondered if he could get past it. Or would each day be another of dread for what could be? She loved him too much to let that happen.

But what were her options? How could they be happy if he were haunted with fear? How could their lives proceed normally when he was so vulnerable? A tear slipped down her cheek.

Zach stirred at the moisture that dampened his chest. "Casey?" He sat up and snapped on the bedside lamp. "You're crying," he announced as she lowered her head.

Casey scrubbed at her cheeks. "It's nothing."

His strong hand gently cupped her chin and lifted her face upward. "Tell me. Us? The baby? Talk to me, Casey."

The confusion couldn't be hidden as it showed itself in her expression, made itself heard in her voice as Casey spoke. "I was thinking about our situation."

Zach's hands moved to her shoulders, his voice vibrant as he ordered, "Forget what I said. This child is our miracle. Conceived before I realized that a doctor couldn't play God. There are so many things that can cripple. I've crippled myself with this fear. It has to stop. Our child will come into this world as God intends. We'll deal with things as they come, but this child will be born and it will be loved."

Casey's arms tightened around her husband as she buried her face against his chest. "I love you, Zachary Taylor."

"I love you too, Slugger," he whispered against her hair. "I need you to teach me undaunted optimism."

Casey lifted her head and stared into the compelling blue eyes, managing a shaky grin, "Quite right. The world's best doctor can't possibly be a pessimist."

"I don't know about the world's best, but who knows—maybe I'll make a difference for our child with my research."

"You will make a difference, Zach. I know you will."

A smile found its way through his uncertainty. "*You* already have, my love. You already have."

epilogue

"This place is a madhouse," Zach whispered.

Casey's smile was one of contentment as her hands slipped over her enlarged abdomen. Their family might be small in number, but they certainly made up for it in volume and celebratory spirit.

And now, she was about to give Zach his gift, hopefully in private. If she could hold on until everyone else was in bed. Then she could get him out of the house without taking the entire family along.

"You're awfully quiet. Didn't you like the earrings?"

The emeralds in their antique bases dangled from her lobes as she flicked her head toward him. He'd had the antique earrings adapted for pierced ears. "They're perfect. Even Stacey loves them."

"I love you," he whispered, the urgency having changed none in the months past. "How can I ever tell you how glad I am that you didn't give up on us?"

She grabbed his hands with such firmness that Zach's head jerked up, his eyes taking in the emotion that burned in her huge brown eyes. "Zach, the New Year is in a few days. Let's start ours tonight. Promise to never mention the time we spent apart again."

"I'd love that."

"Then Happy New Year, darling."

Zach kissed her, his hand moving ever so gently over her abdomen. "How's this fellow doing tonight? Enjoying the celebration with his assorted relatives?"

More like getting ready to join his family, Casey thought joyously, deciding to wait a few minutes longer before she enlightened her husband. She anticipated the apprehension that would fill the neon blue eyes. It had been there on and off ever since he'd accepted this child would be born.

At times there was fear, but there had been other, more wonderful moments. Casey would never forget his reaction to their baby's first kick. He'd been the same when he saw the sonogram pictures. She thought of how he carried them in his wallet and smiled. Casey truly believed these were the times when the miracle became real for him.

He loved touching her abdomen, feeling the fluttering and then the stronger movements as the baby grew within the confines of her body. Once the baby started moving, Zach kept her laughing with the incredible things he said their son was doing. Her favorite had been the Bordeaux-Taylor exercise program. For months, her skin tingled when he whispered directions, often having her in tears of laughter as she begged him to stop.

As her petite body grew larger, Zach reassured her, saying the baby's exercise program was keeping her in prime condition, adding she had never been more gorgeous.

Zach pursued counseling and found his situation not uncommon. From the things he'd told her, Casey believed Zach had adjusted his way of thinking and was gradually leaving his fears behind.

"I like the new wallpaper," she said. "Thanks for finishing it before everyone arrived."

"It is nice. Pity the original wasn't in as good a shape as that in the bedroom. But then we were lucky the house was in livable condition. This fellow kept you from doing as much as you wanted," Zach pointed out, patting her abdomen.

"Did you ever feel God led us to this house?" Casey asked.

"Definitely. How else would we have found a place so perfect for our family?"

Casey looked about the beautifully decorated room, her gaze lingering on the ten-foot Christmas tree that stood in the corner. "I don't know where you found the time to do such a great job," she complimented. "The decorations are perfect and the food delicious."

Zach lifted her hand to his lips. "You've converted me, my love. I never thought I would enjoy it so much. Too bad about the Candlelight Tour, though. Maybe next year."

Casey almost laughed at the thought of her husband actually considering participating in the historical homes tour.

"As long as it hasn't interfered with your research."

The pride she'd felt the day he'd been notified he'd received the research grant had been indescribable. Though Zach had never really admitted how important it was to him, Casey understood the need for him to be involved in diabetes research.

She'd made a decision of her own at that point. If he hadn't received the money, she would have done everything in her power to see that he had his chance. She'd tentatively broached the subject with both sets of parents and found them willing to contribute and help with fundraising.

In fact, each had set aside a substantial sum to add to his grant, pushing aside his protests and arguing it was for their family. Their parents understood how close they had come to divorce because of Zach's fears.

"What's wrong, honey?" Zach demanded, instantly alert as her hand tightened about his.

"The labor started early this morning. No," she said,

grabbing his arm before he could jump to his feet. "I don't want anyone waiting it out with us. It's late. Say good night, and we'll get my bag and go to the hospital."

Doubt filled his eyes. "We should tell them."

"We will, my darling," Casey said, her hand curving about his cheek. "Tonight, I need only you. Let them do their bits later."

Zach gave her a quick kiss. "This revelry has worn Casey out," he announced, the disguised apprehension making his voice louder. "Why don't we call it a night and start up again in the morning?"

The group moved in slow motion, everyone picking up paper from the hardwood floor and stopping to talk among themselves. Casey laughed as she watched Zach's foot tap impatiently. She pushed at his arm. "I'm fine. Go call the doctor and get my bag."

Her gaze followed him across the room. His professionalism couldn't protect him now. Casey smiled at Stacey when she dropped onto the sofa beside her.

"You're in labor."

"How did. . .?" Casey broke off with a laugh.

"I just wanted you to know I've got your number. Giving them their first grandchild to make your gift unique," Stacey teased.

"They say homemade is best," Casey teased. "Besides, that's no way to talk about us making you an aunt. Can't you just see yourself?"

"In time. Maybe when the little slugger is a teenager."

"But you'll have your own family by then."

"Your child will always be as special to me as you are," Stacey vowed, hugging her sister tightly. "You be sure Zach knows to call the moment this baby is born. You two are going to have a lot of explaining to do afterward."

"I love you, Stacey. Now do you suppose you can get me out of this house without everyone else knowing?"

"Are you kidding? Leave everything to me." The familiarity of the plotting going on behind the big brown eyes brought a smile to Casey's face. "Let's see now. You're a bit large to put out the window. But I'll think of something."

꧁

Zach wiped Casey's forehead with a cool cloth. Why didn't they do something? She'd been at this too long. Not really. In his doctor's mode, he knew that. But when it came to the husband's, it was a totally different matter.

"He's crowning," the doctor called to them, instructing, "Hold on for just a minute. Okay now, Casey, push."

So much effort for one tiny little elfin, Zach thought, supporting her shoulders as Casey brought their child into the world.

The doctor worked busily for a few minutes, his calm voice sharing the news they waited for. "Congratulations. You have a son. You want to cut the cord, Zach?"

He left her side, the rush of pride that filled him stronger than all the fears in the world as he cradled the baby in his arms. "A boy, Casey! We have a son."

"Zach, you knew that," she protested with a tired smile.

"I *thought* that," he corrected. "You know the pictures were not conclusive."

"Let me see him," she requested. "Oh, he has your hair. Look at the curls. What color are his eyes?"

"Who can tell with them closed like that?" Zach's finger touched at the dark curls before moving on to stroke fingers and toes. "He's perfect," Zach agreed, looking at Casey.

A satisfied smile curved her lips and their gazes locked.

"I knew he would be."

The nurse took the baby, and their gazes followed. Zach turned back to her. "That's why I need you, Casey Bordeaux-Taylor. You see things I refuse to accept. Without you, we might never have had this moment with our child."

"Are you still worried?"

"Yes," he admitted with a proud, full smile. "I'll always worry about the kind of parents we'll be and his health and happiness, but together we can overcome those fears. We'll sandwich them into the happy periods."

"Just live one day at a time, Zach," Casey said, her hand slipping up his arm. "God will take care of the rest."

Zach covered her hand with his, unfettered love reaching out to her with all its power. "Let's name him Grant."

"Grant?" Casey repeated. They had gone through stacks of baby books, but no definite decision had been made.

"The name seems appropriate. It means brave and valorous. Reminds me of you. The spiritual meaning is promised assurance."

"What about Junior? Our dads?"

"They named their children," Zach said, a stubborn glint in his eyes. "I was the first Zachary in the family line."

"Come to think of it, there never was another Casey either. Grant Zachary Taylor. It's a good strong name."

"Casey," he groaned.

She reached to stroke his face. "Accept it, Zach. You were doomed from the moment you did that first double take. Your life has never been the same since." Weary from hours of labor, her eyes sparkled with love and happiness.

"Double take?" he teased. "I prefer to think of it as destiny giving me a swift kick in the seat of the pants before turning the job over to you."

Laughter replaced the fear in his eyes, and Casey knew boundless joy. Their love was going to be forever. And what a wonderful thought that was.

A Letter To Our Readers

Dear Reader:

In order that we might better contribute to your reading enjoyment, we would appreciate your taking a few minutes to respond to the following questions. We welcome your comments and read each form and letter we receive. When completed, please return to the following:

Rebecca Germany, Fiction Editor
Heartsong Presents
PO Box 719
Uhrichsville, Ohio 44683

1. Did you enjoy reading *Double Take?*
   ☐ Very much. I would like to see more books
     by this author!
   ☐ Moderately
     I would have enjoyed it more if _____
     _____
     _____

2. Are you a member of **Heartsong Presents**? Yes ☐ No ☐
   If no, where did you purchase this book? _____
   _____

3. How would you rate, on a scale from 1 (poor) to 5 (superior), the cover design? _____

4. On a scale from 1 (poor) to 10 (superior), please rate the following elements.

   _____ Heroine   _____ Plot

   _____ Hero   _____ Inspirational theme

   _____ Setting   _____ Secondary characters

5. These characters were special because _____

_____

_____

6. How has this book inspired your life? _____

_____

_____

7. What settings would you like to see covered in future
   Heartsong Presents books? _____

_____

_____

8. What are some inspirational themes you would like to see
   treated in future books? _____

_____

_____

9. Would you be interested in reading other **Heartsong
   Presents** titles?   Yes ❑   No ❑

10. Please check your age range:
    ❑ Under 18   ❑ 18-24   ❑ 25-34
    ❑ 35-45   ❑ 46-55   ❑ Over 55

11. How many hours per week do you read? _____

Name _____

Occupation _____

Address _____

City _____ State _____ Zip _____

Women in touch with God!

When I'm On My Knees

A compilation of prayers from a woman's point of view, prayers that emanate from the heart, prayers about friendship, family, and peace. 224 pages, Printed Leatherette, $4\,^{3}/_{16}$" x $6\,^{3}/_{4}$"

When I'm Praising God

This follow-up to the highly-popular book, *When I'm On My Knees*, will encourage women to praise God in any and every situation. A heart-felt collection of prayers, devotional thoughts, poems, and Scripture, *When I'm Praising God* can help readers turn even the trials of life into victories. 224 pages, Printed Leatherette, $4\,^{3}/_{16}$" x $6\,^{3}/_{4}$"

····Hearts♥ng·····

HEARTSONG PRESENTS *TITLES AVAILABLE NOW:*

_HP177 NEPALI NOON, Susannah Hayden

_HP178 EAGLES FOR ANNA, Cathrine Runyon

_HP181 RETREAT TO LOVE, Nancy N. Rue

_HP182 A WING AND A PRAYER, Tracie J. Peterson

_HP185 ABIDE WITH ME, Una McManus

_HP186 WINGS LIKE EAGLES, Tracie J. Peterson

_HP189 A KINDLED SPARK, Colleen L. Reece

_HP190 A MATTER OF FAITH, Nina Coombs Pykare

_HP193 COMPASSIONATE LOVE, Ann Bell

_HP197 EAGLE PILOT, Jill Stengl

_HP198 WATERCOLOR CASTLES, Ranee McCollum

_HP201 A WHOLE NEW WORLD, Yvonne Lehman

_HP202 SEARCH FOR TODAY, Mary Hawkins

_HP205 A QUESTION OF BALANCE, Veda Boyd Jones

_HP206 POLITICALLY CORRECT, Kay Cornelius

_HP209 SOFT BEATS MY HEART, Aleesha Carter

_HP210 THE FRUIT OF HER HANDS, Jane Orcutt

_HP213 PICTURE OF LOVE, Tamela Hancock Murray

_HP214 TOMORROW'S RAINBOW, VeraLee Wiggins

_HP217 ODYSSEY OF LOVE, Melanie Panagiotopoulos

_HP218 HAWAIIAN HEARTBEAT, Yvonne Lehman

_HP221 THIEF OF MY HEART, Catherine Bach

_HP222 FINALLY, LOVE, Jill Stengl

_HP225 A ROSE IS A ROSE, Ruth Richert Jones

_HP226 WINGS OF THE DAWN, Tracie J. Peterson

_HP233 FAITH CAME LATE, Freda Chrisman

_HP234 GLOWING EMBERS, Colleen L. Reece

_HP237 THE NEIGHBOR, Debra White Smith

_HP238 ANNIE'S SONG, Andrea Boeshaar

_HP241 DESTINY, ARIZONA, Marty Crisp

_HP242 FAR ABOVE RUBIES, Becky Melby and Cathy Wienke

_HP245 CROSSROADS, Tracie Peterson and Jennifer Peterson

_HP246 BRIANNA'S PARDON, Gloria Clover

_HP249 MOUNTAINTOP, Lauralee Bliss

_HP250 SOMETHING FROM NOTHING, Nancy Lavo

_HP253 A MERRY HEART, Wanda E. Brunstetter

_HP254 THE REFUGE, Rae Simons

_HP257 TENDER REMEMBRANCE, Una McManus

_HP258 THE ALASKAN WAY, Marilou H. Flinkman

_HP261 RACE OF LOVE, Melanie Panagiotopoulos

_HP262 HEAVEN'S CHILD, Gina Fields

_HP265 HEARTH OF FIRE, Colleen L. Reece

_HP266 WHAT LOVE REMEMBERS, Muncy G. Chapman

(If ordering from this page, please remember to include it with the order form.)

Presents

Great Inspirational Romance at a Great Price!

Heartsong Presents books are inspirational romances in contemporary and historical settings, designed to give you an enjoyable, spirit-lifting reading experience. You can choose wonderfully written titles from some of today's best authors like Veda Boyd Jones, Yvonne Lehman, Tracie Peterson, Debra White Smith, and many others.

When ordering quantities less than twelve, above titles are $2.95 each.
Not all titles may be available at time of order.

Heartsong Presents
Love Stories Are Rated G!

That's for godly, gratifying, and of course, great! If you love a thrilling love story, but don't appreciate the sordidness of some popular paperback romances, **Heartsong Presents** is for you. In fact, **Heartsong Presents** is the *only inspirational romance book club*, the only one featuring love stories where Christian faith is the primary ingredient in a marriage relationship.

Sign up today to receive your first set of four, never before published Christian romances. Send no money now; you will receive a bill with the first shipment. You may cancel at any time without obligation, and if you aren't completely satisfied with any selection, you may return the books for an immediate refund!

Imagine. . .four new romances every four weeks—two historical, two contemporary—with men and women like you who long to meet the one God has chosen as the love of their lives. . .all for the low price of $9.97 postpaid.

To join, simply complete the coupon below and mail to the address provided. **Heartsong Presents** romances are rated G for another reason: They'll arrive *Godspeed!*